K¹² Read Aloud
Treasury

Book Staff and Contributors

Kristen Kinney *Senior Content Specialist*
Alane Gernon-Paulsen *Content Specialist*
Mary Beck Desmond *Senior Text Editor*
Karen Ingebretsen *Text Editor*
Suzanne Montazer *Creative Director, Print and ePublishing*
Jayoung Cho *Senior Visual Designer*
Oltjen Design Associates *Print Visual Designers*
Kim Barcas, Stephanie Shaw Williams *Cover Designers*
Amy Eward *Senior Manager, Writers*
Colleen Line *Senior Project Manager*

Maria Szalay *Senior Vice President for Product Development*
John Holdren *Senior Vice President for Content and Curriculum*
David Pelizzari *Vice President, Content and Curriculum*
Kim Barcas *Vice President, Creative*
Laura Seuschek *Vice President, Instructional Design and Evaluation & Studies*
Aaron Hall *Vice President, Program Management*

Lisa Dimaio Iekel *Production Manager*
John Agnone *Director of Publications*

Credits

All illustrations © K12 unless otherwise noted

Claudine Gévry, 2–7; North South Studios, 8–9; Jason Wolff, 10–21; Jayoung Cho, 22–23; Laura Huliska-Beith, 24–28; North South Studios, 29; Daniel Boris, 30–33; Jayoung Cho, 34–43; North South Studios, 44–51; Neil Sorenson, 52–60; Daniel Boris, 61; Mike Bohman, 62; Sarah Schanze, 63; Valeria Cis, 64–80; North South Studios, 81; Ian Joven, 82–86; Lael Henderson, 87; Jayoung Cho, 88–92; Sarah Schanze, 93; Mike Reed, 94–98; North South Studios, 99; Monica Gutierrez, 100–103; Mike Bohman, 104–105; Linda Bronson, 106–109; North South Studios, 110–111; Mike Reed, 112–115; Gynux, 116–121; Valeria Cis, 122–127; Ian Joven, 128–132; North South Studios, 133; Jason Wolff, 134–141; North South Studios, 142–147; Sarah Schanze, 148–149; Julissa Mora, 150–153; Peter Francis, 154–159; Laura Huliska-Beith, 160–163; Virginia Allyn, 164–167

About K12 Inc.

K12 Inc., a technology-based education company, is the nation's leading provider of proprietary curriculum and online education programs to students in grades K–12. K¹² provides its curriculum and academic services to online schools, traditional classrooms, blended school programs, and directly to families. K12 Inc. also operates the K¹² International Academy, an accredited, diploma-granting online private school serving students worldwide. K¹²'s mission is to provide any child the curriculum and tools to maximize success in life, regardless of geographic, financial, or demographic circumstances. K12 Inc. is accredited by CITA. More information can be found at www.K12.com.

978-1-60153-144-5
Printed by Worzalla, Stevens Point, WI, USA, April 2018

Contents

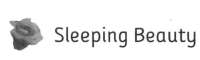 

K¹² Read Aloud

Treasury

Little *Red* Riding Hood

adapted from the Brothers Grimm

Once upon a time, there lived a dear little girl who was loved by everyone. She wore a red velvet cloak and hood everywhere she went, so she was called Little Red Riding Hood.

Early one morning, her mother said, "Little Red Riding Hood, here is a cake and a jug of cider. Take them to your grandmother. She is sick and weak, and they will do her good. Be sure to carry them carefully, and be sure that you do not leave the path."

"I promise," said Little Red Riding Hood. And she set off down the path through the wood to her grandmother's house.

At first she walked very properly and carried the basket carefully. But when she got to the wood, she longed to put down the basket, pick the flowers that smiled up at her, and chase the sunbeams that danced across her path.

Just then a wolf stepped out of the shadows. Little Red Riding Hood did not know what a wicked creature he was, so she was not at all afraid of him.

"Good morning, my dear," said the wolf. "Where are you going on such a fine day?"

"Good morning," Little Red Riding Hood replied politely. "I am taking this basket of cake and cider to my grandmother."

"And where does your grandmother live, my dear?" asked the wolf.

"She lives in a cottage covered with roses, not far from here," said Little Red Riding Hood.

"I see," said the wolf. And then, as he walked by the side of Little Red Riding Hood, the wolf added, "It does seem a shame that you must walk so slowly and carefully when all else in the wood is merry. How sweetly the birds are singing! And look at the pretty flowers! Why not put down your basket and gather some flowers for your kind old grandmother?"

The wolf spoke so sweetly that Little Red Riding Hood forgot her promise not to leave the path. She set down her basket and ran into the wood to pick flowers for her grandmother. But with each flower she picked, she spied another that seemed more beautiful, and dashed deeper and deeper into the wood and farther away from the path.

The wolf laughed as Little Red Riding Hood wandered away from the path. "Ha!" he cried. "I will reach Grandmother's house before Little Red Riding Hood. Then I will gobble up the old woman and have the child for dessert."

The wolf ran straight to Grandmother's house and knocked at the door.

"Who is there?" asked an old voice from within.

"Little Red Riding Hood," replied the wolf in his softest voice. "I bring you cake and cider. Open the door!"

"Lift the latch and come in," called Grandmother. "I am so weak, I cannot get up."

The wolf lifted the latch, the door sprang open, and without saying a word he went straight to Grandmother's bed and swallowed her

up. Then he took one of her frilled nightcaps from a drawer, tied it on his head, and lay down in the bed with the covers tucked tight under his chin.

All this time, Little Red Riding Hood had been running about picking flowers. When she had gathered so many that she could carry no more, she remembered her grandmother and hurried back to the path. She rushed to the rose-covered cottage.

When she arrived at her grandmother's house, she was surprised to see the door standing open. So she stood on the step and called out, "Grandmother, may I come in?"

"Of course, my dear," said the wolf in his softest voice. But his softest voice was still a growl, and Little Red Riding Hood felt uneasy as she walked in.

Little Red Riding Hood drew near the bed. There lay what she thought was her grandmother with her cap pulled far over her face, and looking very strange.

"Oh, Grandmother!" said Little Red Riding Hood, "What big ears you have!"

"The better to hear you with, my dear," was the reply.

"But, Grandmother, what big eyes you have!" she said.

"The better to see you with, my dear."

"But, Grandmother, what a terrible big mouth you have!"

"All the better to eat you with, my dear!"

With that, the wolf threw off the covers, sprang at Little Red Riding Hood, and swallowed her in one big gulp.

With his stomach so full, the wolf felt tired, so he lay down again and fell fast asleep. Soon he began to snore—*very* loudly.

Just then, a woodman passed by the cottage. "How the old woman is snoring!" he said to himself. "I must see if she is all right."

When he entered the cottage, he saw the wolf lying on the bed. "It's you, you wicked creature!" he exclaimed. "I have been looking for you for a long time."

He raised his ax, but then he thought that the wolf might have eaten the grandmother and that she might still be saved. So, since the wolf was sleeping so soundly, with his mouth wide open as he snored, the woodman reached down into the wolf's belly. Imagine his surprise as he pulled and out came Little Red Riding Hood!

"How frightened I have been!" the little girl cried. "How dark it was inside the wolf!"

Then out came Grandmother, too, for the wolf had swallowed them so quickly that his great teeth had not touched them.

The wolf woke with a start, and, seeing the woodman with his ax, the wolf ran from the cottage, never to be seen again.

Grandmother ate the cake and drank the cider that Little Red Riding Hood had brought, and soon she felt much better.

But Little Red Riding Hood only said to herself, "As long as I live, I will listen to my mother, and never again leave the path to run into the wood." ❧

One, Two, Buckle My Shoe

One, two,
Buckle my shoe.

Three, four,
Shut the door.

Five, six,
Pick up sticks.
Seven, eight,
Lay them straight.

Nine, ten,
A big fat hen.

Eleven, twelve,
Dig and delve.

Thirteen, fourteen,
Maids a-courting.

Fifteen, sixteen,
Maids in the kitchen.

Seventeen, eighteen,
Maids in waiting.

Nineteen, twenty,
My plate's empty.

Jack and
the Beanstalk

adapted from the retelling by James Baldwin

There was once a boy named Jack, who lived with his mother in a small house at the end of a field. They were so poor that it was hard for them to get food to eat and clothes to wear. All that they had in the world was a red cow that they kept for her milk.

One day Jack's mother said, "Jack, the rent must be paid this week or else we shall be put out of doors. There's not a cent in the house. You must take the cow to town and sell her for as much as you can get."

So Jack tied a rope to one of the cow's horns and set out to take her to town. He had not gone far when he met a man with a wrinkled face and sharp gray eyes.

"My boy, whose cow is that?" said the man.

"She is my mother's cow," said Jack, "and I am taking her to town to sell her."

"Ah!" said the man, "and how much will you take for her?"

"As much as I can get," said Jack.

Then the man showed him five beans and said, "I will give you these beans for your cow."

Jack had never seen such beans. One was white, one was red, one was blue, one was brown, and one was black. He looked at them a long time and thought how nice it would be to take them home and show them to his mother. As to how they could help her pay the rent— well, he did not think of that.

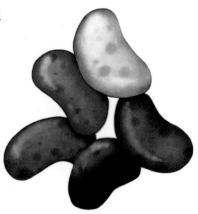

"All right!" he said to the man at last. "You may have the cow."

With the five beans in his hand, he ran back home as fast as he could go.

"Are you back so soon, Jack?" said his mother. "How much did you get for the old cow?"

"Guess," said Jack.

"Oh, tell me! I cannot guess," said his mother.

"Well," said Jack, "I met a man on the road, and he gave me these five beans for the old cow." And he showed the beans to his mother.

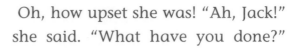

Oh, how upset she was! "Ah, Jack!" she said. "What have you done?" Then she snatched the beans from his hand and threw them out the window. "Now," she shouted, "off to bed with you! You shall not have a bite to eat this night. And don't let me hear a word from you!"

Jack climbed up to his little room, fell into bed, and went to sleep.

When he awoke, his little room looked so strange and shady that he could not think where he was. Where sunlight usually poured through the window, only one or two beams trickled in.

He jumped out of bed and dressed himself quickly. What, he wondered, were those green leaves in front of the window? There had never been anything like them there before.

He looked out the window and saw they were the leaves of a beanstalk. The five beans had sprouted and grown overnight into the biggest beanstalk that anybody ever saw. It went up and up and up, to the very sky. Why, who wouldn't give a cow for beans that would make such a stalk as that?

The beanstalk was so close to the window that Jack stepped out among its branches. And then, since it looked so much like a ladder, he began to climb. He climbed, and he climbed, and he climbed, till at last he was in the sky. His mother's house looked like a tiny speck way down below, but he did not want to climb back down till he had taken a look around.

At the top of the beanstalk, he found a broad, smooth road. "I might as well walk a little way and see where this road goes," said Jack to himself.

He had not gone far when he came to a big tall house. A big tall woman with red hair stood on the steps.

"You there," she said to Jack. "You'd better go back."

But Jack only replied, "Good morning, ma'am. I've come a long way, and I'm very tired. Will you be so kind as to give me a bit of breakfast, and let me rest in your house a little while?"

"Breakfast!" echoed the big tall woman. "If it's breakfast you're wanting, it's breakfast you'll likely be, for I expect my man home any moment. Don't you know my man is a giant? And there's nothing he likes better for breakfast than a fat boy grilled on toast."

Jack, who was not a bit of a coward, replied cheerfully, "I'd be fatter if I'd had my breakfast!"

At which the giant's wife laughed and told Jack to come in, for she had a kind heart. She took Jack into the kitchen, and gave him all the bread and cheese that he could eat. He was just eating the last mouthful when he heard a great noise in the hallway—*thump! thump! thump! thump!*

"Ah, here comes my man now!" cried the woman. "Get in here, quick, for if he finds you, he will eat you up!"

She opened the oven door and pushed Jack inside, where he would be out of sight. And she was just in time, for the giant came into the room the very next minute—*thump! thump! thump! thump!*

He was a very large man and very tall. He looked so mean and fierce that even Jack trembled in the oven.

The giant had three sheep strung to his belt, and he threw them down on the table. "Here, wife," he growled, "this is all I've been able to get this morning. Roast me these for breakfast, and be quick about it. Is the oven good and hot?"

As the giant approached the oven, Jack sat still as a mouse, wondering what would happen next.

"Roast these scrawny things?" cried the giant's wife. "Pooh! These little things would dry to cinders in the oven. Better that I boil them."

So she set to work to boil them. But the giant frowned horribly and said, "What's this I smell? What's this I smell?" Then he went thumping round the room, looking very cross and fierce. At last he stopped right in front of the oven and cried out,

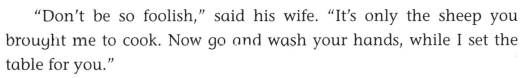

Fee-fi-fo-fum,
I smell the blood of an Englishman.
Be he alive, or be he dead,
I'll grind his bones to make my bread.

"Don't be so foolish," said his wife. "It's only the sheep you brought me to cook. Now go and wash your hands, while I set the table for you."

So off the giant went—*thump! thump! thump! thump!*—to the well at the back of the house. There was a great tub of water there, and he was soon busy washing his hands and combing his long hair. Jack thought that it would be a good time to slip out of the oven and run away. But the big tall woman told him to keep still.

"Wait till after my man has eaten his breakfast," she said. "He will go to sleep in his chair, and then you can run away."

And so the giant sat down to his breakfast. How he did eat! The three boiled sheep made him only a few mouthfuls, and a loaf of bread was only a small bite. After he had finished, he said to his wife, "Now fetch me the hen I took last week, and be quick about it!"

The big tall woman went out, and soon came back with a beautiful hen in her arms. Jack peeped out of the oven to see what the giant was going to do. Was he going to eat the hen, too? No—he put it on the table before him and gently stroked its back. Then he said, "Lay!" and the hen laid an egg of gold. He stroked it again and said, "Lay!" and it laid another egg all of gold.

Soon there was a plateful of golden eggs on the table. By and by, the giant began to nod, and then his eyes closed, and he began to snore.

"Now you may come out of the oven and run away," said the woman to Jack.

Jack crept out and looked around him. "I wish I had such a hen as that," he said.

"Well," said the woman, "the hen is no more his than it is yours, so take it if you will. But don't make a noise!"

Jack climbed up and took the hen off the table. Then he leaped down and ran as fast as his legs could carry him. But just as he got out of the house, the hen cackled and woke the giant.

"Wife, wife," cried the giant, "where is my golden hen?"

And that was all Jack heard, for he rushed down the road and scurried down the beanstalk to his mother's house, all before the giant had time to snap his fingers.

"See what I have brought you from the top of the beanstalk," he said to his mother.

Then he showed her the wonderful hen and told it to lay, and it laid an egg all of gold. Of course his mother was pleased, and she forgot all about the red cow that Jack had sold for five beans.

The little hen laid a golden egg for Jack every time he said "Lay!" The rent was paid, and Jack and his mother lived very comfortably.

It wasn't long till Jack wanted to try his luck with the giant again.

One fine morning, he rose very early and began to climb the beanstalk. He climbed, and he climbed, and he climbed, until he thought he would never get to the top. It seemed to be so much higher than before, but at last he was in the land of the sky, and he saw the road running straight toward the place where the giant lived.

But this time the road seemed much longer than before, and he walked, and he walked, and he walked, until the sun was setting in the west. Then at last he came to the same big tall house, and the same big tall woman was standing on the steps.

"You'd better go back," she said.

But Jack begged that she would give him a bite to eat and let him rest in her house a little while.

"Are you the lad to whom I gave the golden hen?" she said.

"I am," said Jack.

"Well," said the big tall woman, "my man has been ever so angry since you left. He's always stomping around and roaring about how he would like to catch and eat every boy he might find."

While Jack was eating bread and cheese in the kitchen, the giant came home—*thump! thump! thump!* He seemed to be in a great rage, and he roared,

Fee-fi-fo-fum,
I smell the blood of an Englishman.
Be he alive, or be he dead,
I'll grind his bones to make my bread.

Jack just had time to creep into the breadbox and pull the lid down after him when the giant came into the room.

"Where is the boy, wife?" he said.

"What boy?" she asked.

"The boy that took the golden hen," he said. "I smell him, I smell him! He must be here!"

"He hid in the oven the other time," said his wife. "Look for him there."

The giant rushed to the oven and looked in. But he found nothing there except a few big loaves baking.

"There!" said his wife. "What's the good of all your *fee-fi-fo-fums*? It's only the bread that you smell. Come, sit down at the table and eat your supper."

So the giant sat down and ate his supper. But he was cross. When he finished, he said, "Wife, fetch me my harp, and be quick about it!"

The woman brought the most beautiful harp that Jack had ever seen. She set it down on the table before him, and the giant said to it, "Sing!" Then the cords of the harp began to tremble, and sweet, wonderful music came from them as if they were touched by fairy fingers.

The giant listened to the music for a long time, and Jack peeped out from the top of the breadbox and listened, too. By and by, the giant began to nod, and then his eyes closed, and he snored so loudly that the harp stopped its music and did not play any more.

"Now, you'd better run back home," said the woman to Jack.

Jack crept out of the breadbox and looked around. "I wish I had such a harp as that," he said.

"It is yours," said the woman, who had grown fond of Jack. "But be quick and quiet about it," she added.

Jack took the harp in his arms and ran. But just as he got to the door the harp began to play music.

The giant woke up with a start, and Jack rushed away. The harp kept playing loudly. The giant hurried out and saw Jack far down the road. But the big fellow had eaten and drunk so much that he could not run fast. He roared in great rage, and his voice sounded like thunder among the clouds.

Jack was halfway down the beanstalk when the giant got to the top. At first the big fellow was afraid to step down among the branches, so he stood there shaking his fist and roaring till Jack had almost reached the ground.

Then the giant swung himself down among the branches of the beanstalk and began to slide toward the ground. The branches were in his way a good deal, and he couldn't move very fast.

"Mother! mother!" cried Jack. "Bring me the hatchet! Bring me the hatchet!"

His mother ran out with the hatchet. But when she came to the foot of the beanstalk, she was frightened almost to death, for she saw the giant coming down and heard his angry voice like thunder among the clouds.

Jack took the hatchet and began to chop at the beanstalk. Soon it trembled and shook, and then it toppled over, and fell with a great crash among the rocks and trees. Of course the giant came tumbling down with it. Some say that was the end of the giant, but Jack has always claimed that the giant still lives in the big tall house in the land of the sky—though of course no one can go and see, for there is no beanstalk to climb.

And so, with the golden eggs from the hen, Jack and his mother always had plenty of food to eat and clothes to wear. They built themselves a fine new house to live in, where the harp played lovely music for them all day long. And they even bought back the red cow and brought her home again. ᪥

Old *Mother* Hubbard

Old Mother Hubbard
Went to the cupboard,
To get her poor dog a bone;
But when she came there,
The cupboard was bare,
And so the poor dog had none.

She took him a clean dish
To get him some tripe;
But when she came back,
He was smoking a pipe.

She went to the hatter's
To buy him a hat;
But when she came back,
He was feeding the cat.

She went to the barber's
To buy him a wig;
But when she came back,
He was dancing a jig.

She went to the tailor's
To buy him a coat;
But when she came back,
He was riding a goat.

She went to the cobbler's
To buy him some shoes;
But when she came back,
He was reading the news.

This wonderful dog
Was Dame Hubbard's delight;
He could sing, he could dance,
He could read, he could write.

The
Gingerbread
Man

One day an old woman was making gingerbread cookies. Her little boy watched her. She made a Gingerbread Man for him.

She put sugar on the head for hair. She put in two raisins for eyes. Then she went out to call the old man to his dinner.

She said to her little boy, "Stay here and watch the oven to make sure the cookies do not burn. And watch the Gingerbread Man. We do not know what he may do."

Well, the boy watched the oven for a while. But, by and by, he went out to get a drink of water.

As soon as the boy was out the door, the Gingerbread Man hopped out of the pan, jumped out of the oven, and was down on the floor. The boy heard him and ran back as fast as he could. He tried to shut the door.

But he was not in time.

In a minute the Gingerbread Man was through the door and out in the yard. He ran through the yard. He ran out into the road, and he kept running as fast as he could go.

The boy ran after him. He called to his mother. The old woman saw what had happened, and she ran, too.

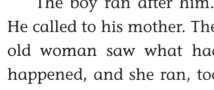

The old man saw them, and he ran as fast as he could. But they could not run fast enough. They could not catch the Gingerbread Man.

The Gingerbread Man ran on and on. Soon he came to two farmers. "Wait a minute," they cried. "You look good enough to eat. Come here, and we will eat you."

But the Gingerbread Man did not stop. As he ran, he called out,

> Run, run, as fast as you can.
> You can't catch me,
> I'm the Gingerbread Man!
> I've outrun a woman,
> A boy, and a man.
> I can outrun you,
> I'm sure that I can.

Down the road he ran. The farmers ran behind him as fast as they could. But they could not catch him.

The Gingerbread Man ran on and on. He came to two puppies by the road. First they saw him, and then they sniffed him. He smelled good enough to eat.

"Wait a minute," they said. "You smell good enough to eat. Wait, so that we can eat you."

But the Gingerbread Man ran on. He called back:

> Run, run, as fast as you can.
> You can't catch me,
> I'm the Gingerbread Man!
> I've outrun two farmers,
> As fast as they ran,
> A little old woman,
> A boy, and a man.
> I can outrun you, too,
> I'm sure that I can.

Down the road ran the Gingerbread Man. The puppies ran after him. They ran as fast as they could.

They ran until their legs were tired. But they could not run fast enough to catch the Gingerbread Man.

The Gingerbread Man ran on and on. By and by, he came to a fox. The fox was lying close by the road. He did not move. He called to the Gingerbread Man, "Good morning. You seem to be in a hurry. Where are you going so fast?"

The Gingerbread Man stopped for a minute. He wanted to hear what the fox said.

"You are a fine runner," said the fox. "Where are you going so fast?"

Then the Gingerbread Man said:

> *Run, run, as fast as you can.*
> *You can't catch me,*
> *I'm the Gingerbread Man!*
> *I've outrun the puppies,*
> *And farmers who ran,*
> *A little old woman,*
> *A boy, and a man.*
> *I can outrun you, too,*
> *I'm sure that I can.*

"Oh," said the fox, "I see. It's those fine legs of yours. I think I never saw such fine legs. Please come closer. Let me see those fine legs. Don't be in such a hurry."

The Gingerbread Man came closer.

"Do come closer," said the fox. "You are so fast. I'm sure I can't outrun you."

The Gingerbread Man came closer to the fox. Then the fox gave one jump and one bite with his teeth.

And that was the end of the Gingerbread Man! 🍂

Hey, Diddle, Diddle

Hey, diddle, diddle,
The cat and the fiddle,
The cow jumped over the moon.
The little dog laughed to see such sport
And the dish ran away with the spoon.

The *Wheels* on the *Bus*

The wheels on the bus go round and round,
Round and round,
Round and round.
The wheels on the bus go round and round,
All through the town.

The wipers on the bus go swish, swish, swish,
Swish, swish, swish,
Swish, swish, swish.
The wipers on the bus go swish, swish, swish,
All through the town.

The doors on the bus go open and close,
Open and close,
Open and close.
The doors on the bus go open and close,
All through the town.

The driver on the bus says, "Move on back!
Move on back!
Move on back!"
The driver on the bus says, "Move on back!"
All through the town.

The babies on the bus say, "Waa, waa, waa,
Waa, waa, waa,
Waa, waa, waa."
The babies on the bus say, "Waa, waa, waa,"
All through the town.

The mommies on the bus say, "Shh, shh, shh,
Shh, shh, shh,
Shh, shh, shh."
The mommies on the bus say, "Shh, shh, shh,"
All through the town.

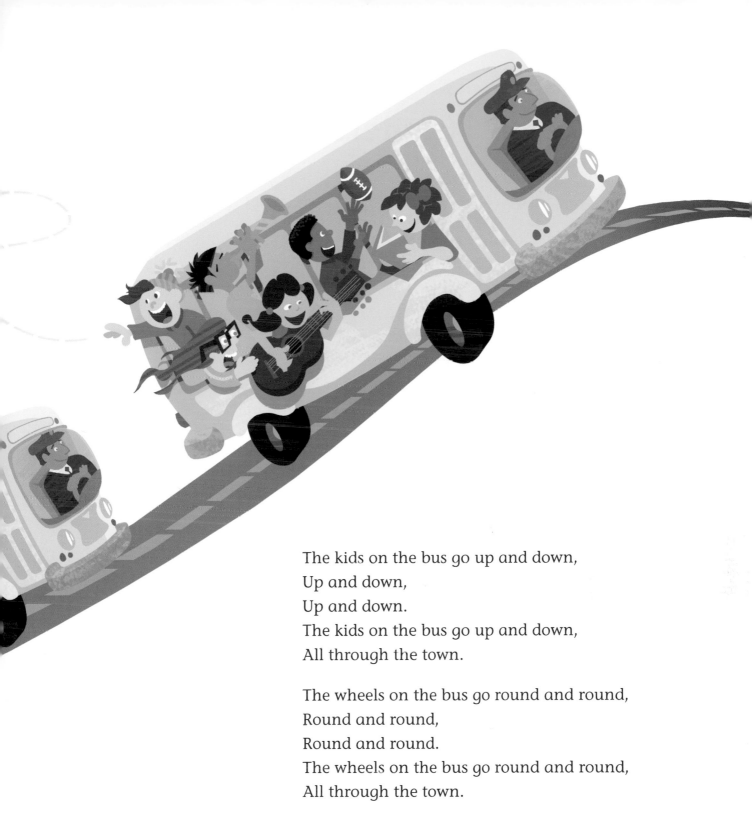

The kids on the bus go up and down,
Up and down,
Up and down.
The kids on the bus go up and down,
All through the town.

The wheels on the bus go round and round,
Round and round,
Round and round.
The wheels on the bus go round and round,
All through the town.

Cinderella

adapted from Charles Perrault

Once upon a time, there lived a fair young girl with her father and mother in a beautiful home in the city. She was as happy as she was good, and she had all that her heart could wish.

But by and by, a sad day came, and then many sad days. Her mother fell ill and died. Then, some time after, her father married again. But the stepmother was cross and unkind. And, to make matters worse, she had two daughters of her own who were as cross and unkind as she. They were so idle and selfish that they made the poor young girl do all the work about the house.

She swept the floors and scrubbed the stairs and made the beds and cooked the dinner and washed the dishes. And when all the housework was finished, she had to wait on her two proud stepsisters, make their

fine dresses, and brush their hair when they went to bed. They slept in fine rooms where there were big, soft beds, and long mirrors in which they could see themselves from head to foot. But she was sent to lie on an old pile of straw in the attic where there was only one broken chair.

And when her day's work was done, they made her sit in the chimney corner among the ashes and cinders, and called her Cinderella, the cinder maid. But even dirtied with dust and cinders, she was far more beautiful than they.

It happened at this time that the Prince, whose father was King of that country, was nearly twenty-one years old. To celebrate his birthday, a splendid ball was to be given at the royal palace. Invitations were sent out far and wide. Cinderella's stepsisters went wild with delight when they received an invitation. They were proud and happy, imagining what they would wear. For days and days they talked of nothing but clothes.

"I am going to wear my blue velvet dress, and trim it with fine lace," said the elder stepsister.

"And I am going to wear my pink satin, with diamonds and pearls," said the younger stepsister.

But the ball only meant more work for Cinderella. She had to wash

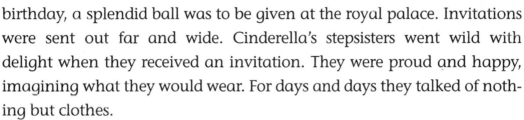

her stepsisters' dresses, iron their laces, press their ribbons, and put their ruffles in order. And when they quarreled over who would look more beautiful, it was Cinderella who made peace between them.

In the evening, while she brushed and braided their hair, the elder stepsister said, "Cinderella, don't you wish you were going to the ball tonight?"

"Oh, you are only teasing me," she replied. "It is not for me to go to so fine a place as that."

"You are quite right," snapped the younger stepsister. "Who would ask a dusty little ash-sweeper to go to a royal ball? You're only fit to dance with your broom!"

Cinderella said nothing, and only kept arranging their braids and curls.

At last, the stepsisters were ready, and the carriage came clattering to the door. They climbed in and were whisked away to the ball.

Cinderella watched the carriage until it disappeared from sight. Then she sat down by the kitchen fire and cried.

As Cinderella wept and sobbed, she heard a kind voice say, "Dry your tears, my dear, and tell me what the matter is."

Cinderella looked up to see her godmother, who was a fairy, standing before her.

"I wish I could—I wish—," sobbed Cinderella.

"I know," said her godmother kindly. "You want to go to the ball, don't you?"

"Y-yes," said Cinderella.

"Well now," said her fairy godmother, "I know you are a good girl, and so, let us see what we can do. Come now, run into the garden, and fetch me a pumpkin."

Cinderella wondered how a pumpkin could help her go to the ball, but she ran outside and soon returned with the finest pumpkin she could find. Her godmother scooped out the inside and then tapped it with her wand. Suddenly the pumpkin grew into a fine golden coach lined with red satin, while its curling vines looped themselves into four delicate wheels.

Then her godmother noticed seven fat mice in the mousetrap. "Lift the trap door," she said.

Cinderella did, and as the mice scurried out, her godmother touched them with her wand and turned them into six prancing horses. The last and biggest mouse, she turned into a fat, jolly coachman with a fine set of long whiskers.

"Now, dear," she said, "go into the garden and bring me the two green lizards behind the watering can."

Cinderella carried the lizards back to her godmother, who touched each one with her wand and turned them into footmen, their green uniforms sparkling with silver and gold. They leapt up behind the carriage and stood waiting there as if they had been footmen all their lives.

Then her godmother said, "Here is a carriage fit to take you to the ball. Are you pleased with it?"

"Oh, yes," cried Cinderella. And she was about to leap into the coach when she thought of the rags she was wearing. "Oh, but dear Godmother," she said, "What shall I do about my clothes?"

Her godmother laughed and touched Cinderella with her wand. The girl's ragged frock became a rich dress of gold and silver, spangled with jewels every color of the rainbow.

Then Cinderella asked, "And, Godmother, how shall I dance?" She pointed to her bare toes, which peeped from beneath her beautiful dress.

"Goodness me, I quite forgot the shoes!" said her godmother. And then she took out of her pocket the most delicate pair of little glass slippers, which fit Cinderella perfectly.

"Oh, Godmother! How can I ever thank you?" cried Cinderella.

"Never mind about thanking me," said her godmother. "Only remember to do exactly as I say. You must leave the ball before twelve o'clock. If you stay a moment after midnight, the coach will turn

back into a pumpkin, the horses and coachman will become mice, the footmen will turn to lizards, your beautiful dress will vanish, and only your rags will be left behind."

"I promise, Godmother, I will return before midnight," said Cinderella as she stepped into the golden coach. The coachman cracked his whip, the footmen jumped up behind, and the six fine horses galloped away like the wind.

When Cinderella arrived at the palace, the Prince himself ran to welcome her. He gave her his hand as she stepped out of the coach. When they entered the hall, the music stopped, the people fell silent, and all eyes turned to Cinderella. "How beautiful she is!" they whispered to each other. The King himself whispered to the Queen that he had never seen so fair a maiden.

Then the music struck up again, and the Prince led Cinderella out to dance. She danced so gracefully that everybody thought her even lovelier than before.

All night long the Prince would dance with no one but Cinderella. She was so happy that she forgot to look at the clock. And before she had stayed even half as long as she wished, she heard the clock begin to strike twelve.

At once, Cinderella remembered her godmother's warning, and she rose up and ran from the room. But as she hurried down the steps, one of her glass slippers came off.

As the clock rang out the last strokes—nine, ten, eleven, twelve—the coach became a pumpkin again, and the mice and lizards scampered away into the shadows. As Cinderella hurried out through the great gate, her beautiful dress turned back into her old, ragged frock.

Moments later, the Prince arrived. He asked the guards if they had seen a princess pass that way. The guards replied, "We saw only a poor girl in rags, Your Highness."

Then the Prince went back, shaking his head sadly, for he did not know the name of the beautiful stranger with whom he had danced all night. All he had was the shining glass slipper she had left behind.

Cinderella ran through the night and finally returned home, tired and cold. Of her godmother's gifts, all she had left was one glass slipper. She took it off and tucked it carefully into her pocket. Then she sat down by the fire to wait for her stepsisters to return.

"Sitting among the ashes as usual," they cried when they came in. "Come, be quick, and help us get ready for bed."

As Cinderella hung up their dresses and brushed their hair, her stepsisters chattered about the ball.

"There were so many beautiful ladies there," said the elder stepsister, "but of course none as beautiful as we were—except perhaps a strange princess who danced all night with the Prince."

"But she acted so strangely!" broke in the younger stepsister. "Did you see, when the clock struck twelve, she ran away without bidding anybody good night?"

"Cinderella!" snapped the elder stepsister. "Are you listening at all? Off to bed with you! You look as if you were dreaming already."

Cinderella climbed the stairs to her wretched bed in the attic. The next day, she was back at work, sweeping and scrubbing as hard as ever.

Meanwhile, the Prince could think of no one but the lovely stranger whose name he did not know. He sent men all through the land to invite every young lady to try on the little glass slipper. And he declared that he would marry the one whose foot the slipper fit.

The glass slipper was placed on a purple velvet cushion and carried around to every house, so that each lady might try it on.

When the messenger arrived at the house where Cinderella lived, the proud stepsisters were so excited that their hands trembled.

"I shall try it on first," said the elder.

"No, my foot is smaller than yours," cried the younger, and they pushed each other very rudely.

The elder stepsister snatched the slipper and began to try it on. She pushed and tugged till her face grew red. But not even her toes would fit in the delicate glass slipper.

Then the younger stepsister took it. She managed to squeeze her toes in, but the heel would not go on.

"Silly thing! I don't believe it was meant to be worn," she cried, as she kicked it off and burst into tears.

As the messenger picked up the slipper, a quiet voice said, "Please, may I try it on?"

"Cinderella!" screeched the elder stepsister. "How dare you come in here!"

"You try on the slipper, indeed!" cried the younger. "No cinder maid's rough foot could fit in that delicate thing."

But the messenger bowed to Cinderella and offered her the slipper upon the velvet cushion. "It is the Prince's command that every maiden in the land may try on the slipper," he said.

So Cinderella sat down, and he put the slipper on her foot. It fit perfectly. Then from her pocket she drew the other slipper, and put it on her other foot.

At that moment, her fairy godmother appeared. She touched Cinderella with her wand, and Cinderella was no longer a cinder maid, but a beautiful young lady dressed in silk and satin.

The stepsisters recognized her as the lovely princess whom they had seen at the ball. They threw themselves at her feet and asked her to forgive them for the unkind way they had treated her. She said that she forgave them, and wished them always to love her.

Soon after, the Prince and Cinderella were married, and they lived happily together for many, many years. As for her stepsisters, Cinderella gave them rooms in the palace. They left off their cross, ugly ways, and, by and by, married two gentlemen of the court. For from their stepsister, they had learned that far more important than a fine dress and a fancy hairdo are a kind heart and a generous spirit.

Sleeping Beauty

adapted from the Brothers Grimm

Once upon a time, there lived a good king, and a queen who was as gentle as she was beautiful. They loved each other dearly and ruled together over a peaceful kingdom. Still, they were very sad, for they did not have a child. They longed for a son or daughter more than anything in the world.

The queen grew sadder and sadder, and could think of nothing else, until one day she went to bathe in the cool water of the fountain, when a frog suddenly jumped out and sat at the edge gazing at her.

"You shall have your wish," he croaked. "This very time next year, when the briar rose begins to flower, a living rosebud shall blossom for you."

And the next year, just at the time of the roses, the queen had a little baby daughter, just as the frog had said. And they named the baby Briar-Rose.

To celebrate, the king ordered a great feast and invited everyone he knew, including kings and queens from lands near and far, as well as dozens of princes and princesses. But the most honored guests of all were the fairies, for each of them would give a magical gift to little Briar-Rose.

There were 13 fairies in the kingdom, but the king had only 12 gold plates. The king did not want to anger one of the fairies by giving her a wooden plate. So he sent out 12 invitations to the fairies, and planned to send the thirteenth after he ordered his craftsmen to make one more gold plate. But in all the hustle and bustle of preparing for the great feast, the king quite lost track of what he had planned to do, and soon forgot the matter entirely.

The feast day came. The guests arrived, all dressed in jewels and velvet. The bells rang out, and the fairies stood around the cradle to give their gifts to Briar-Rose.

"Happiness will shine down on her like sunbeams," said the first fairy.

"She will be wise and thoughtful," said the second.

"She will be good and kind-hearted," said the third.

"She will dance with grace and play sweet music," said the fourth.

One by one, the fairies gave Briar-Rose their gifts, until, at last, the twelfth fairy stepped forward.

But before she could speak, the doors burst open and the thirteenth fairy stormed into the hall. She looked so angry that everyone drew back to let her pass.

The fairy went straight to the baby's cradle and shrieked, "You shall have my gift, Briar-Rose, though I was not invited to the feast! When you are 15 years old, you shall prick your finger on the spindle of a spinning wheel and fall down dead."

Then she cast an evil look all round, and flew out the window.

Everyone stood wide-eyed and silent, except the twelfth fairy, who said, "Do not be afraid. I still have my gift to give. I cannot undo what has been done, but I can soften the evil. My gift is this. The princess Briar-Rose will not die when she pricks her finger on the spindle. Instead, she will fall into a deep sleep that will last a hundred years."

The king was so anxious to guard his dear child that he sent a hundred men to gather all the spinning wheels in the kingdom. He piled the spinning wheels in the courtyard, burned them to ashes, and said, "From this day forth, no one in the kingdom may have a spinning wheel. Then our dear Briar-Rose will be safe."

Briar-Rose grew up blessed by the fairies' gifts. She was clever and good, and as happy as the day was long. The king and queen forgot about the thirteenth fairy's evil words, and the years slipped by until Briar-Rose turned 15.

Not long after her fifteenth birthday, Briar-Rose was wandering about the castle, while the king and queen were away in the countryside. She wandered from room to room until she came to an old tower. Curious, she climbed the narrow, winding staircase to the small door at the top.

A rusty key was in the lock. When she turned it, the door sprang open, and there in a little room sat an old woman with a spindle, busily spinning her white yarn.

"Oh, what a funny thing that is!" said Briar-Rose, looking at the spinning wheel, for she had never seen such a thing before. "How I would love to make it go whirling round and round!"

47

As soon as she reached out her hand, the thirteenth fairy's words came true. Briar-Rose pricked her finger on the spindle. But, as the twelfth fairy had promised, she did not die. Instead, she sank down and fell into a deep sleep.

At that moment, everyone and everything in the castle stopped what they were doing and fell fast asleep, too. The king and queen, who had just returned and were walking through the hall, sank down into two soft chairs, and the king, it must be admitted, began to snore rather loudly. The guards fell asleep where they stood at the gates. The cook in the kitchen, who was just preparing to dip her ladle into a steaming pot of soup, went fast asleep with her hand still in the air.

As for the cat, she was already fast asleep, as usual, by the kitchen fire. But then the fire stopped crackling and burning, the pots stopped boiling, nothing stirred, nothing moved, not a sound was heard. Only around the castle there sprung up a hedge of briar-roses that grew taller and taller, until the castle was quite hidden. Not even the flags on the highest towers could be seen.

As the years went by, people began to forget about the castle. Only the old people would sometimes tell the children about the Sleeping Beauty, a beautiful princess who once lived in a castle where the briar roses grew. But the children thought it was a make-believe story, for the hedge was so thick and high that no one could see what was inside.

From time to time, a prince would come riding by and hear the tale, and he would try to cut through the thorny hedge, hoping to find the castle with the Sleeping Beauty. But the thorns clawed and tore at every man who tried to cut through the hedge, and each year, the hedge grew taller and thicker.

Now it happened that on the very day when the princess had been asleep for a hundred years, there came to that country a prince who was braver and kinder than any of the princes who had come before. He had heard the story of the princess Briar-Rose, and made up his mind to find her.

"The thorns in the hedge will tear you to pieces," all the people said.

"I am not afraid," said the prince. "I shall not return until I win my way through."

And so he rode bravely to the great hedge, and prepared to cut his way through with his sword. All at once, however, the hedge blossomed with pale pink roses. The branches parted in front of him to make a passage, and the thorns turned themselves away. He walked along a grassy avenue until he came to the edge of the castle. Not a sound broke the stillness; not a leaf whispered in the breeze.

The prince walked past the guards, who still stood asleep on their feet. He entered the castle and saw the king and queen asleep in their chairs. Everyone and everything was the same as when they had fallen asleep a hundred years ago.

Then the prince noticed the steps that led to the tower. He climbed the steps, just as Briar-Rose had done so long ago. And when he opened the door and stepped inside, he stood still in wonder.

The princess lay there fast asleep. Her fair face was turned toward him, just as she had sunk down to rest a hundred years before. Everything was the same, except that around the couch had grown a canopy of briar-roses to protect her as she slept. The flowers perfumed the air, and the sharp thorns guarded her from harm.

So beautiful did the princess look lying there, like a pale rose herself, that the prince was drawn to her side; and, bending over her, he kissed her cheek.

The princess's eyelids quivered and opened. She looked up and gave a little gasp of joy.

"You have come at last," she cried. "I have been dreaming and dreaming of you for such a long time."

Now, the moment Briar-Rose opened her eyes, everyone and everything else in the castle began to awake, too. The king and queen arose and walked down the hall. The guards shook themselves and stood straight at their posts. The horses chewed their hay, the pigeons strutted about on the roof, the fire blazed, the pots boiled, and the

wind whistled merrily around every corner. Even the cat stood to stretch and yawn before curling herself back up for another nap by the fire.

Then, with a sound like a deep sigh, the great hedge of briar roses sank down and down until it vanished in the earth. Not even a petal was left.

"It does not matter that the roses are gone," said the prince, "for I have found my own Briar-Rose, who is fairest of them all."

And so they were married, and lived happily ever after. ᧞

Rapunzel

adapted from the Brothers Grimm

Once upon a time, there lived a man and his wife who were unhappy because they had no children. After many years, however, it seemed that their great wish was to come true, because at last they were about to have a child.

Each day, as the wife went about her work, she would stop from time to time to gaze out a little window at the back of the cottage. Through the window she could see a beautiful garden, full of the finest vegetables and flowers. But, as much as she wanted to, she could not go inside, because the garden was surrounded by a high wall, and belonged to a powerful witch, whom the whole world feared.

Then one morning, the wife noticed a new bed of fresh greens, called rapunzel, planted in the garden. The leaves looked so tender and green that she longed to eat them. Her longing increased day by day, until she would do nothing but gaze out the window and dream of tasting the rapunzel in the witch's garden. And because she knew she could not have any of it, she turned pale and thin, until her husband became quite worried and asked, "What is the matter, dear wife?"

"Oh," said she, "if I cannot have some of the rapunzel from the witch's garden, I will surely die!"

The man loved his wife very much, and he said to himself, "I will not let my wife die. Whatever may happen, I will get her some of the witch's rapunzel."

That evening, when darkness fell, the man climbed over the wall into the garden. He grabbed a handful of green rapunzel leaves and brought them back to his wife. At once, she made a salad of them, and ate until every last leaf was gone.

But she liked it so much, and it tasted so good, that the next day she longed for it even more. So again her husband waited until dark, climbed over the wall into the garden, and grabbed a handful of the green leaves. But as he turned to go, he drew back in terror, for there, standing before him, was the old witch.

"Did you think you could climb into my garden and steal my rapunzel?" she shrieked. "You will pay dearly for it!"

"Have mercy!" the man cried. "My wife saw your rapunzel through her window, and now she will eat nothing else. She has grown so thin, I am afraid she and the child she carries will die if I do not bring her some."

The witch said, "If that is true, take as much rapunzel as you like. But you must promise me that when the child is born, you will give it to me. Do not be afraid, for I will treat it well and care for it like a mother."

The poor man was so frightened that he promised everything, and on the day the child was born, the witch appeared at the door to claim it. There was nothing the man and his wife could do.

"I will call her Rapunzel," said the witch, and she took the baby away with her.

Rapunzel grew up to be as bright and lovely as a summer's day. But when she turned 12 years old, the witch took her to the darkest

corner of the forest and shut her up in a tower. The tower had no steps and no door. It had only one tiny window near the top. So when the witch wished to be let in, she would stand below the window and cry,

*Rapunzel, Rapunzel,
let down your hair!*

Rapunzel had beautiful long hair that shone like gold. When she heard the witch's voice, she would open the window and let her braids fall to the witch waiting below. The witch would grasp one braid in each hand, and climb up the side of the tower.

55

So the days passed, until a few years later, when a prince happened to come riding through the forest. As he wandered past the tower, he heard a voice singing so sweetly that he stood still and listened. It was Rapunzel, passing the lonely hours singing sad songs.

The prince wanted to meet the lovely singer, so he rode round and round the tower, searching for a door. Finding none, he turned and rode

sadly home. But her song had touched his heart, and every day he returned to the forest to listen to it.

One day, as he was standing in the shadow of a great tree listening to Rapunzel sing, he saw the witch approach the tower, and then he heard her cry,

Rapunzel, Rapunzel,
let down your hair!

He watched Rapunzel let down her golden hair, and saw the witch climb up to the window. He said to himself, "If that is the ladder that one must climb, then I will try it myself."

The next day, as soon as it grew dark, he went to the tower and cried,

Rapunzel, Rapunzel,
let down your hair!

And she let down her braids, and the prince climbed up them, and into the little room.

When Rapunzel saw the prince, she moved backward in fright, for she had never seen a man before. But the prince spoke to her kindly. "Do not be afraid," he said. "I have heard you sing such sad songs, and I wish only to make them happy ones, if you will let me."

The prince spoke so gently that Rapunzel forgot her fear, and when at length he asked her to marry him, she said, "Yes," and she laid her hand in his.

Then she told him, "When you come again to see me, bring me silk thread. I can weave a ladder. When the ladder is ready, I will climb down from the tower, and we will ride away together."

They agreed that he should visit her only in the evenings, for the witch came to the tower only in the day. And so it went for many days, and the old witch knew nothing. But then one day, Rapunzel, not thinking of what she was saying, asked the witch, "How is it that you are so much heavier to pull up than the young prince?"

"The prince?" shrieked the witch. "I thought I had hidden you from all the world. You wicked child, you have betrayed me!"

In her fury, she grabbed Rapunzel's thick braids in one hand and a pair of scissors in the other, and—snip! snip!—the beautiful braids fell in a heap upon the floor. Then she dragged Rapunzel to a lonely wilderness, a place of rock and ruin, and left the poor girl there alone and miserable.

That evening, the witch returned to the tower and fastened Rapunzel's braids to a hook beside the window. Soon, the prince came and called,

Rapunzel, Rapunzel,
let down your hair!

The witch let down the braids, and the prince climbed up them, and into the little room.

"Aha!" sneered the witch, springing out of the shadows. "You came for your darling, but the sweet bird sits no longer in the nest, and sings no more. Rapunzel is lost to you; you will never see her again!"

The prince gasped and stumbled backwards. In his haste, he slipped on the stones and fell out of the window, landing in the thorn bushes at the bottom of the tower.

He struggled out of the brambles, but the thorns had cut his eyes, and he could no longer see. From that day on, he wandered blindly through the forest, eating nothing but roots and berries, and weeping for the loss of his dear bride-to-be.

After years of wandering, the prince at last reached the wilderness where the witch had taken Rapunzel. He heard a sweet voice singing in the distance—and the voice seemed so familiar! He followed the song, and when he approached, Rapunzel knew him at once. She ran to him, cradled him in her arms, and wept.

And as she wept, two of her tears bathed his eyes, and they became clear again, and he could see as well as ever.

The prince led Rapunzel home to his kingdom, where they were received with great joy, and where they were married and lived long and happily together. ❧

Old **King** Cole

Old King Cole
Was a merry old soul,
And a merry old soul was he.
He called for his pipe,
And he called for his bowl,
And he called for his fiddlers three.

Baa Baa, Black Sheep

Baa baa, black sheep
Have you any wool?
Yes, sir, yes, sir,
Three bags full.

One for the master,
And one for the dame,
And one for the little boy
Who lives down the lane.

Baa baa, black sheep
Have you any wool?
Yes, sir, yes, sir,
Three bags full.

Jack Be
Nimble

Jack be nimble,

Jack be quick,

Jack jump o v e r

the candlestick.

The *Velveteen* Rabbit

by Margery Williams

There was once a velveteen rabbit, and in the beginning he was really splendid. He was fat and bunchy, as a rabbit should be; his coat was spotted brown and white, he had real thread whiskers, and his ears were lined with pink sateen. On Christmas morning, when he sat wedged in the top of the Boy's stocking, with a sprig of holly between his paws, the effect was charming.

There were other things in the stocking—nuts and oranges and a toy engine, and chocolate almonds and a clockwork mouse. But the Rabbit was quite the best of all. For at least two hours the Boy loved him, and then aunts and uncles came to dinner, and there was a great rustling of tissue paper and unwrapping of parcels. In the excitement of looking at all the new presents, the Velveteen Rabbit was forgotten.

For a long time he lived in the toy cupboard or on the nursery floor, and no one thought very much about him. He was naturally shy, and being only made of velveteen,

some of the more expensive toys quite snubbed him. The mechanical toys were very superior, and looked down upon everyone else; they were full of modern ideas, and pretended they were real. The model boat, who had lived through two seasons and lost most of his paint, caught the tone from them. So he never missed an opportunity of referring to his rigging in technical terms. The Rabbit could not claim to be a model of anything, for he didn't know that real rabbits existed. He thought they were all stuffed with sawdust like him, and he understood that sawdust was quite out-of-date and should never be mentioned in modern circles. Even Timothy, the jointed wooden lion, who was made by the disabled soldiers and should have had broader views, put on airs and pretended he was connected with Government. Among them all, the poor little Rabbit was made to feel very insignificant and commonplace. The only person who was kind to him at all was the Skin Horse.

The Skin Horse had lived longer in the nursery than any of the others. He was so old that his brown coat was bald in patches and showed the seams underneath, and most of the hairs in his tail had been pulled out to string bead necklaces. He was wise, for he had seen a long succession of mechanical toys arrive to boast and swagger, and by and by, break their mainsprings and pass away. He knew that they were only toys, and would never turn into anything else. For nursery magic is very strange and wonderful, and only those playthings that are old and wise and experienced like the Skin Horse understand all about it.

"What is *Real*?" asked the Rabbit one day, when they were lying side by side near the nursery fender, before Nana came to tidy the room. "Does it mean having things that buzz inside you and a stick-out handle?"

"Real isn't how you are made," said the Skin Horse. "It's a thing that happens to you. When a child loves you for a long, long time, not just to play with, but *really* loves you, then you become Real."

"Does it hurt?" asked the Rabbit.

"Sometimes," said the Skin Horse, for he was always truthful. "But when you are Real, you don't mind being hurt."

"Does it happen all at once, like being wound up," he asked, "or bit by bit?"

"It doesn't happen all at once," said the Skin Horse. "You *become* Real. It takes a long time. That's why it doesn't often happen to toys that break easily, or have sharp edges, or who have to be carefully kept. Generally, by the time you are Real, most of your hair has been loved off, and your eyes drop out, and you get loose in the joints and very shabby. But these things don't matter at all, because once you are Real you can't be ugly, except to people who don't understand."

"I suppose *you* are Real?" said the Rabbit. And then he wished he had not said it, for he thought the Skin Horse might be sensitive. But the Skin Horse only smiled.

"The Boy's Uncle made me Real," he said. "That was a great many years ago; but once you are Real you can't become unreal again. It lasts for always."

The Rabbit sighed. He thought it would be a long time before this magic called Real happened to him. He longed to become Real, to know what it felt like; and yet the idea of growing shabby and losing his eyes and whiskers was rather sad. He wished that he could become it without these uncomfortable things happening to him.

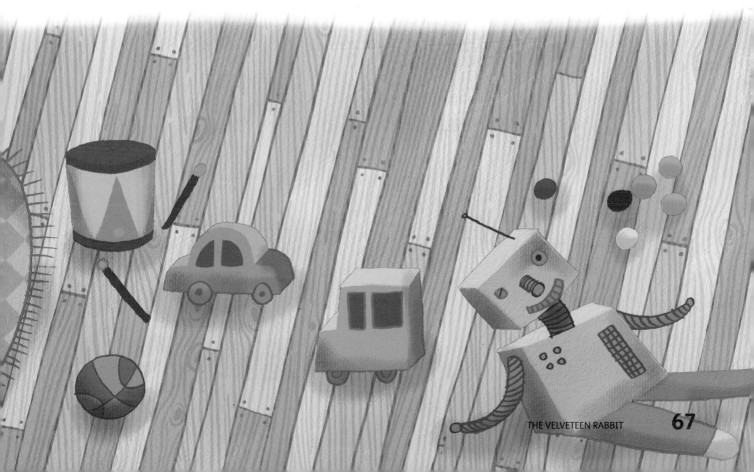

There was a person called Nana who ruled the nursery. Sometimes she took no notice of the playthings lying about. But sometimes, for no reason whatever, she went swooping about like a great wind and hustled them away in cupboards. She called this "tidying up," and the playthings all hated it, especially the tin ones. The Rabbit didn't mind it so much, for wherever he was thrown he came down soft.

One evening, when the Boy was going to bed, he couldn't find the china dog that always slept with him. Nana was in a hurry, and it was too much trouble to hunt for china dogs at bedtime, so she simply looked about her, and seeing that the toy cupboard door stood open, she made a swoop.

"Here," she said, "take your old Bunny! He'll do to sleep with you!" And she dragged the Rabbit out by one ear, and put him into the Boy's arms.

That night, and for many nights after, the Velveteen Rabbit slept in the Boy's bed. At first he found it rather uncomfortable, for the Boy hugged him very tight, and sometimes he rolled over on him, and sometimes he pushed him so far under the pillow that the Rabbit could scarcely breathe. And he missed, too, those long moonlight hours in the nursery, when all the house was silent, and his talks with the Skin Horse. But very soon he grew to like it, for the Boy used to talk to him, and made nice tunnels for him under the bedclothes that he said were like the burrows the real rabbits lived in. And they had splendid games together, in whispers, when Nana had gone away to her supper and left the night-light burning on the mantelpiece. And when the Boy dropped off to sleep, the Rabbit would snuggle down close under his little warm chin and dream, with the Boy's hands clasped close round him all night long.

And so time went on, and the little Rabbit was very happy—so happy that he never noticed how his beautiful velveteen fur was getting shabbier and shabbier, and his tail becoming unsewn, and all the pink rubbed off his nose where the Boy had kissed him.

Spring came, and they had long days in the garden, for wherever the Boy went the Rabbit went, too. He had rides in the wheelbarrow, and picnics on the grass, and lovely fairy huts built for him under the raspberry canes behind the flower border. And once, when the Boy was called away suddenly to go out to tea, the Rabbit was left out on the lawn until long after dusk. Nana had to come and look for him with the candle because the Boy couldn't go to sleep unless he was

there. He was wet through with the dew and quite earthy from diving into the burrows the Boy had made for him in the flowerbed, and Nana grumbled as she rubbed him off with a corner of her apron.

"You must have your old Bunny!" she said. "Fancy all that fuss for a toy!"

The Boy sat up in bed and stretched out his hands.

"Give me my Bunny!" he said. "You mustn't say that. He isn't a toy. He's *Real*!"

When the little Rabbit heard that, he was happy, for he knew that what the Skin Horse had said was true at last. The nursery magic had happened to him, and he was a toy no longer. He was Real. The Boy himself had said it.

That night he was almost too happy to sleep, and so much love stirred in his little sawdust heart that it almost burst. And into his boot-button eyes, that had long ago lost their polish, there came a look of wisdom and beauty, so that even Nana noticed it next morning when she picked him up, and said, "I declare if that old Bunny hasn't got quite a knowing expression!"

That was a wonderful summer!

Near the house where they lived there was a wood, and in the long June evenings the Boy liked to go there after tea to play. He took the Velveteen Rabbit with him, and before he wandered off to pick flowers, or play at brigands among the trees, he always made the Rabbit a little nest somewhere among the bracken, where he would be quite cozy. He was a kind-hearted little boy, and he liked Bunny to be comfortable. One evening, while the Rabbit was lying there alone, watching the ants that ran to and fro between his velvet paws in the grass, he saw two strange beings creep out of the tall bracken near him.

They were rabbits like him, but quite furry and brand new. They must have been very well made, for their seams didn't show at all, and they changed shape in a queer way when they moved. Instead of always staying the same like he did, one minute they were long and thin, and the next minute fat and bunchy. Their feet padded softly on the ground, and they crept quite close to him, twitching their noses, while the Rabbit stared hard to see which side the clockwork stuck out. He knew that toys that jump generally have something to wind them up. But he couldn't see it. They were evidently a new kind of rabbit altogether.

They stared at him, and the little Rabbit stared back. And all the time their noses twitched.

"Why don't you get up and play with us?" one of them asked.

"I don't feel like it," said the Rabbit, for he didn't want to explain that he had no clockwork.

"Ho!" said the furry rabbit. "It's as easy as anything." And he gave a big hop sideways and stood on his hind legs.

"I don't believe you can!" he said.

"I can!" said the little Rabbit. "I can jump higher than anything!" He meant when the Boy threw him, but of course he didn't want to say so.

"Can you hop on your hind legs?" asked the furry rabbit.

That was a dreadful question, for the Velveteen rabbit had no hind legs at all! The back of him was made all in one piece, like a pincushion. He sat still in the bracken, and hoped that the other rabbits wouldn't notice.

"I don't want to!" he said again.

But the wild rabbits have very sharp eyes. And this one stretched out his neck and looked.

"He hasn't got any hind legs!" he called out. "Fancy a rabbit without any hind legs!" And he began to laugh.

"I have!" cried the little Rabbit. "I have got hind legs! I am sitting on them!"

"Then stretch them out and show me, like this!" said the wild rabbit. And he began to whirl round and dance, until the little Rabbit got quite dizzy.

"I don't like dancing," he said. "I'd rather sit still!"

But all the while he was longing to dance, for a funny new tickly feeling ran through him, and he felt he would give anything in the world to be able to jump about like these rabbits did.

The strange rabbit stopped dancing, and came quite close. He came so close this time that his long whiskers brushed the Velveteen Rabbit's ear, and then he wrinkled his nose suddenly and flattened his ears and jumped backwards.

"He doesn't smell right!" he exclaimed. "He isn't a rabbit at all! He isn't real!"

"I *am* Real!" said the little Rabbit. "I am Real! The Boy said so!" And he nearly began to cry.

Just then there was a sound of footsteps, and the Boy ran past near them, and with a stamp of feet and a flash of white tails the two strange rabbits disappeared.

"Come back and play with me!" called the little Rabbit. "Oh, do come back! I *know* I am Real!"

But there was no answer, only the little ants ran to and fro, and the bracken swayed gently where the two strangers had passed. The Velveteen Rabbit was all alone.

"Oh, dear!" he thought. "Why did they run away like that? Why couldn't they stop and talk to me?"

For a long time he lay very still, watching the bracken, and hoping that they would come back. But they never returned, and presently the sun sank lower and the little white moths fluttered out, and the Boy came and carried him home.

Weeks passed, and the little Rabbit grew very old and shabby, but the Boy loved him just as much. He loved him so hard that he loved all his whiskers off, and the pink lining to his ears turned gray, and his brown spots faded. He even began to lose his shape, and he scarcely looked like a rabbit anymore, except to the Boy. To him he was always beautiful, and that was all that the little Rabbit cared about. He didn't mind how he looked to other people, because the nursery magic had made him Real, and when you are Real shabbiness doesn't matter.

And then, one day, the Boy was ill.

His face grew very flushed, and he talked in his sleep, and his little body was so hot that it burned the Rabbit when he held him close.

Strange people came and went in the nursery, and a light burned all night. Through it all the little Velveteen Rabbit lay there, hidden from sight under the bedclothes. He never stirred, for he was afraid that if they found him someone might take him away, and he knew that the Boy needed him.

It was a long weary time, for the Boy was too ill to play, and the little Rabbit found it rather dull with nothing to do all day long. But he snuggled down patiently, and looked forward to the time when the Boy should be well again. They would go out in the garden amongst the flowers and the butterflies and play splendid games in the raspberry thicket like they used to. All sorts of delightful things he planned, and while the Boy lay half asleep he crept up close to the pillow and whispered them in his ear. Presently the fever turned, and the Boy got better. He was able to sit up in bed and look at picture books, while the little Rabbit cuddled close at his side. And one day, they let him get up and dress.

It was a bright, sunny morning, and the windows stood wide open. They had carried the Boy out onto the balcony, wrapped in a shawl, and the little Rabbit lay tangled up among the bedclothes, thinking.

The Boy was going to the seaside tomorrow. Everything was arranged, and now it only remained to carry out the doctor's

orders. They talked about it all, while the little Rabbit lay under the bedclothes, with just his head peeping out, and listened. The room was to be disinfected, and all the books and toys that the Boy had played with in bed must be burnt.

"Hurrah!" thought the little Rabbit. "Tomorrow we shall go to the seaside!" For the boy had often talked of the seaside, and he wanted very much to see the big waves coming in, and the tiny crabs, and the sand castles.

Just then Nana caught sight of him.

"How about his old Bunny?" she asked.

"*That*?" said the doctor. "Why, it's a mass of scarlet fever germs!—Burn it at once. What? Nonsense! Get him a new one. He mustn't have that anymore!"

And so the little Rabbit was put into a sack with the old picture books and a lot of rubbish, and carried out to the end of the garden behind the fowl-house. That was a fine place to make a bonfire, only the gardener was too busy just then to attend to it. He had the potatoes to dig and the green peas to gather, but next morning he promised to come early and burn the whole lot.

That night the Boy slept in a different bedroom, and he had a new bunny to sleep with him. It was a splendid bunny, all white plush with real glass eyes, but the Boy was too excited to care very much about it. For tomorrow he was going to the seaside, and that in itself was such a wonderful thing that he could think of nothing else.

And while the Boy was asleep, dreaming of the seaside, the little Rabbit lay among the old books in the corner behind the fowl-house, and he felt very lonely. The sack had been left untied, and so by wriggling a bit he was able to get his head through the opening and look out. He was shivering a little, for he had always been used to sleeping in a proper bed. By this time his coat had worn so thin and threadbare from hugging that it was no longer any protection to him.

Nearby he could see the thicket of raspberry canes, growing tall and close like a tropical jungle, in whose shadow he had played with the Boy on bygone mornings. He thought of those long sunlit hours in the garden—how happy they were—and a great sadness came over him. He seemed to see them all pass before him, each more beautiful than the other: the fairy huts in the flower-bed, the quiet evenings in the wood when he lay in the bracken and the little ants ran over his paws; the wonderful day when he first knew that he was Real. He thought of the Skin Horse, so wise and gentle, and all that he had told him. Of what use was it to be loved and lose one's beauty and become Real if it all ended like this? And a tear, a real tear, trickled down his little shabby velvet nose and fell to the ground.

And then a strange thing happened. For where the tear had fallen a flower grew out of the ground, a mysterious flower, not at all like any that grew in the garden. It had slender green leaves the color of emeralds, and in the center of the leaves was a blossom like a golden cup. It was so beautiful that the little Rabbit forgot to cry, and just lay there watching it. And presently the blossom opened, and out of it, there stepped a fairy.

She was quite the loveliest fairy in the whole world. Her dress was of pearl and dewdrops, and there were flowers round her neck and in her hair, and her face was like the most perfect flower of all. And she came close to the little Rabbit and gathered him up in her arms and kissed him on his velveteen nose that was all damp from crying.

"Little Rabbit," she said, "don't you know who I am?"

The Rabbit looked up at her, and it seemed to him that he had seen her face before, but he couldn't think where.

"I am the nursery magic Fairy," she said. "I take care of all the playthings that the children have loved. When they are old and worn out and the children don't need them anymore, I come and take them away with me and turn them into Real."

"Wasn't I Real before?" asked the little Rabbit.

"You were Real to the Boy," the Fairy said, "because he loved you. Now you shall be Real to everyone."

And she held the little Rabbit close in her arms and flew with him into the wood.

It was light now, for the moon had risen. All the forest was beautiful, and the fronds of the bracken shone like frosted silver. In the open glade between the tree trunks the wild rabbits danced with their shadows on the velvet grass. But when they saw the Fairy they all stopped dancing and stood round in a ring to stare at her.

"I've brought you a new playfellow," the Fairy said. "You must be very kind to him and teach him all he needs to know in Rabbit-land, for he is going to live with you forever and ever!"

And she kissed the little Rabbit again and put him down on the grass.

"Run and play, little Rabbit!" she said.

But the little Rabbit sat quite still for a moment and never moved. For when he saw all the wild rabbits dancing around him he suddenly remembered about his hind legs, and he didn't want them to see that he was made all in one piece. He did not know that when the Fairy kissed him that last time she had changed him altogether. And he might have sat there a long time, too shy to move, if just then something hadn't tickled his nose, and before he thought what he was doing, he lifted his hind toe to scratch it.

And he found that he actually had hind legs! Instead of dingy velveteen he had brown fur, soft and shiny, his ears twitched by themselves, and his whiskers were so long that they brushed the grass. He gave one leap and the joy of using those hind legs was so great that he went springing about the turf on them, jumping sideways and

whirling round as the others did. He grew so excited that when at last he did stop to look for the Fairy, she had gone.

He was a Real Rabbit at last, at home with the other rabbits.

Autumn passed and then winter. In the spring, when the days grew warm and sunny, the Boy went out to play in the wood behind the house. While he was playing, two rabbits crept out from the bracken and peeped at him. One of them was brown all over, but the other had strange markings under his fur, as though long ago he had been spotted, and the spots still showed through. And about his little soft nose and his round black eyes there was something familiar, so that the Boy thought to himself:

"Why, he looks just like my old Bunny that was lost when I had scarlet fever!"

But he never knew that it really was his own Bunny, come back to look at the child who had first helped him to be Real.

Jack
Sprat

Jack Sprat could eat no **fat**,
His wife could eat no lean.
And so between the two of them
They licked the platter clean.

The **Lion** and the **Mouse**

adapted from a fable by Aesop

Once a great, big lion lay fast asleep in the woods. By and by, a mouse came along, a little, teeny, tiny mouse. Now, the lion was lying so still that the mouse thought he was only a big heap of dried brown grass. So the mouse began scampering around, up and down the lion's body.

The little feet of the mouse were tickling the lion's stomach. The lion opened one big, round eye and then he opened the other. He saw the teeny, tiny mouse and he woke up wide awake! "Grrr!" growled the lion. He reached out a paw and *snap!* He snatched the little mouse.

"So," the lion roared, "it's you who've awakened me! I'll put a stop to that! I'll eat you for my breakfast!"

The mouse was terribly frightened. His heart went pit-a-pat, but he squeaked in a wee, little voice, "Oh, mighty king of the beasts, please don't eat me! If you'll let me go this once, I'll never forget your kindness!"

But the lion opened his great big mouth and began to smack his lips. "Yum, yum, little mouse," he said. "I think you'll taste very good."

Trembling all over, the mouse pleaded, "Please let me go! Oh, please! Who knows, great king of the beasts, if you let me go, it might happen that someday I could be helpful to you!"

"You help me!" cried the lion. "A teeny, tiny thing like you, help the great king of the beasts! Ha ha! Hee hee! Ho ho!" He laughed so loud and so long that all the forest rang. But all this laughing made the lion feel very jolly. "Well, after all," he said, "you're really too small to make a good breakfast!" So the lion opened his great, big paw, and the little mouse slipped out as fast as he could to hide himself in the grass.

Not long after this, the lion was wandering in the woods. Suddenly he fell in a hole that had been dug by some hunters who wanted to catch the lion.

The lion was groaning in the deep hole when the hunters found him. With a strong net they drew him up out of the trap and then tied him with a rope to a tree. "Oh ho," they laughed, "let us go and fetch a strong cage for this lion."

"I must get away," thought the lion, "before the hunters come back!" And he tugged and tore at the rope, but he could not get himself free. And so at last he cried sadly, "They have me! I cannot get loose! I shall end my life in a cage! Nevermore shall I roam free in this great, beautiful forest!"

But as he was crying and sighing, it chanced that the mouse came by, the teeny, tiny, little mouse.

"Oh, friend lion," he squeaked. "What has happened to you, the great king of the beasts?"

"The hunters have tied me up," the lion groaned. "There isn't a thing I can do to break this great, strong rope."

"Oh, is that all your trouble, friend?" said the mouse with a laugh.

"You needn't seem so glad about it," the lion grumbled. "It's a very sad end for me!"

But already the little mouse had gone straight to the rope and begun to gnaw it with his sharp teeth. He gnawed and he gnawed and he gnawed. And pretty soon *split, split, split,* the rope began to break. Bit by bit, the mouse chewed until all at once, *snip, snap,* he had gnawed through the very last strand. The rope broke apart and there stood the lion, free!

"You thought I could never help you," the little mouse said to the lion, "but look, I have set you free!"

The lion was so surprised he could hardly speak. "Well, well!" he said at last. "Just look at what you've done! A teeny, tiny thing like you has set free the king of the forest! I'm ashamed that I laughed at you. You've shown me that, no matter how very small one is, he can always be helpful to others. Goodbye, little friend! I thank you!"

And with a great, happy roar, the lion bounded into the forest. ꙮ

Three **Blind** **Mice**

Three blind mice!
See how they run!
They all ran after the farmer's wife,
Who cut off their tails with a carving knife.
Did you ever see such a thing in your life
As three blind mice?

The *Elves* and *the* Shoemaker

Once upon a time, a shoemaker lived in a little town. He was a good man and worked hard, but he became too poor to buy more leather. At last he had only enough leather left to make one pair of shoes. At night he cut out the leather, but it was too late to finish making the shoes. So, he put the pieces on his bench and went to bed with a sad heart.

In the morning, when he went to finish the shoes, what did he find? They were all done! Done inside, and done outside!

Now this surprised the good man. His eyes grew bigger and bigger. Who in the world, he wondered, could have finished the shoes?

"Wife," he called, "the shoes are done! Come and see."

So she ran to see. Sure enough, there were the shoes, all done. Then her eyes grew bigger and bigger. *Who* could have finished the shoes?

While they were wondering, in came a customer. "Have you any shoes to sell?" he asked.

"One pair, sir," said the shoemaker, and he showed the pair on the bench.

"These are very fine shoes," said the customer. "I will pay you very well for them."

After the happy customer left with the shoes, the shoemaker had money to buy enough leather to make two more pairs of shoes. He cut out the new leather that night.

"I will finish these shoes in the morning," he said. "Come, wife, it is late. Let us go to bed."

The next morning, the shoemaker went to his bench, and what do you think he found? There were the two pairs of shoes, all finished! He and his wife wondered and wondered. *Who* could have been kind enough to finish the shoes?

While they were wondering, in came two customers.

"Have you any shoes to sell?" they asked. "Two pairs, sirs," said the shoemaker, and he showed them the two pairs on the bench.

"Ah, these are fine shoes, indeed," said one customer.

"The finest I ever saw!" said the other customer. "Let us pay a good price for them."

When the happy customers paid the shoemaker, he had money to buy enough leather for four more pairs of shoes.

This kept going on, day after day, night after night. Each night, the shoemaker cut out the leather. Each morning, he found finished shoes waiting for him. Each day, his customers paid him a high price.

At last he began to be rich. But still he did not know who was making his shoes.

One night he called to his wife. "Let us sit up tonight," he said. "We can hide behind the door. Then we can see who makes the shoes."

"Good!" said the wife. "Let us do so. I, too, want to see who is helping us."

That night, after the pieces of leather were cut out, the old people hid behind the door and peeped through the crack. By and by, in ran two little elves, dressed in ragged clothes. They were no bigger than your hand. *Skippety hop!* They ran to the bench. They picked up the shoes. Then, *rappety rap!* Oh, how they worked! In no time the shoes were finished. Then, *hoppety skip*, away they went again!

The old people rubbed their eyes to see if it was true. Yes, it was. For there were the shoes, all finished.

The next day the shoemaker's wife said, "The little elves have been very kind to us. Let us do something to make them glad. Let us give them some new clothes. I will make the clothes, and you can make some little shoes."

So the good woman sewed all day. She made two little blue suits and several little white shirts. Last of all, she knitted two wee pairs of short red stockings. The shoemaker made two tiny pairs of shoes. At night they put the new things on the bench. Then they hid behind the door again.

The clock struck twelve. In skipped the two little elves. Up they jumped to the shoemaker's bench. But they found no pieces of

leather. Instead, they found the new clothes and little shoes waiting for them. *Whisk*, off went the old clothes! And *whoosh*, on went the new! Then the little men danced for joy. They danced and skipped from the bench. They skipped and danced over the floor. Then they danced out of the door, singing these words:

> *"Happy little elves are we,*
> *Neatly dressed, as you can see,*
> *No more shoemakers to be."*

No one saw them again, but from that day the shoemaker had good luck. His heart was never sad again. He always had money for leather, and his customers paid him well.

So you must know that good luck will come wherever the elves have danced. But they never dance where people are bad or lazy. ✤

The Little Elf

by John Kendrick Bangs

I met a little Elf-man once,
Down where the lilies blow.
I asked him why he was so small,
And why he didn't grow.
He slightly frowned, and with his eye
He looked me through and through.
"I'm quite as big for me," said he,
"As you are big for you."

Spider *and* Turtle
and **Good Manners**

Turtle had crawled all day long for many miles. He was hungry and thirsty when the sun started to set. Then he smelled something good.

Down a hill, he could see Spider's web and his camp. Spider was cooking ten potatoes in his fire. The smell made Turtle hungry. He crawled as fast he could to Spider's camp.

"Hello, Anansi!" he said. (*Anansi* was the name of the spider.) Anansi said, "Hello, Turtle! What do you want? I'm busy and ready to have my supper."

Turtle said, "I am so hungry. Can you share your potatoes with me?"

"Of course!" said Anansi. But he really wanted to keep all his potatoes for himself. On the outside, he smiled. Inside, he kept thinking and thinking.

Turtle rolled a potato out of the fire. Anansi the Spider cleared his throat. "Ahem!" he said. "I am glad to share, but I believe in good manners. I see that the toenails on your feet are dirty.

We spiders do not like our guests to eat with dirty nails. We are delicate like our webs and we have dainty manners. Please go to the creek to wash first."

Turtle felt bad. "I am sorry, Anansi," he said, "you are right. Guests should show good manners when they accept free food."

Spider pointed with one of his eight legs. "There's a little creek not too far away," he said. "You can wash over there. If you don't mind, I'll begin eating while I'm waiting for you to come back."

Turtle crawled to the creek as fast as he could. He couldn't go too fast, because he was a turtle. Meanwhile, Spider began eating. He ate five potatoes before Turtle came back.

"I've washed my toenails now," said Turtle. Then he rolled a potato out of the fire. "Ahem!" said Spider, "Your feet still look dirty to me." Spider was right. Turtle's toenails had gotten dirt in them

again when he crawled back from the creek. Turtle blushed, and went back to wash again in the creek.

When Turtle returned, Spider had eaten four more potatoes. Turtle reached for the last one. "Ahem, ahem!" said Spider, "You don't know how to clean your toenails well. They are still dirty. Please wash them again."

Ashamed, Turtle crawled away to wash again. Spider ate up the last potato. When Turtle came back, Spider burped loudly. "Well, my friend," he said, "you have taken so long to clean up that there are no potatoes left."

Turtle looked straight into Spider's eyes. "You have tricked me," he said. "You began by offering to share your food with me when I was hungry. So, out of good manners, I will make you the same offer if you ever come to my house. Still, I will remember that your good manners hid a trick." Spider laughed, and Turtle crawled away.

Many months passed. For a while, Spider caught many good things to eat in his web, but soon there came a long spell with no rain. Spider was going hungry. He thought about Turtle's offer to share his food. "Turtle lives by a river. Even during a dry spell, it will still be a little bit wet and there will be good things to eat. I'll visit him."

Spider put on his coat and ran on his eight legs to the river where Turtle lived. There he saw Turtle ready to slide into the water.

"Hello, Turtle! I was in the neighborhood," said Spider.

"Well, Anansi. It's been a long time since I've seen you. Every time my stomach has growled, I have thought of you. But it's not growling tonight, because I have a nice meal planned at the bottom of the river where I live. Please dive down to join me." Then Turtle slid into the river.

"Oh, thank you!" said Spider. He tried to dive down to follow Turtle to the bottom. But a spider is so light that he kept rising to the top, like a bubble.

Spider wondered how to get to the bottom. He saw some gleaming pebbles on the riverbank. "Aha!" he thought. "To sink, I'll fill the

eight pockets on my coat with pebbles. To rise, I'll take the pebbles out. I can put Turtle's food in my pockets."

Spider picked up eight pebbles, one for each leg. He put them in his eight pockets on his eight sleeves. Then he jumped into the river and sank to the bottom. He found Turtle at his table eating his dinner. Spider started to grab dinner with his two front legs. Turtle stopped him.

"You said spiders were dainty and delicate in their manners," said Turtle. "I took off my coat for dinner. So should you. If you leave it on, it looks like you want to eat and run. We turtles think that's bad manners. We don't eat and run because we don't run. I hope you will show me good manners since I'm sharing my food with you."

Spider was caught. He took off his coat, leg by leg by leg by leg by leg by leg by leg by leg. As soon as the coat was all the way off, it dropped with the sound of eight banging pebbles. Spider popped up to the surface like a bubble. He grabbed a reed with two of his legs. He looked back down into the water. Turtle was laughing and enjoying his big meal all by himself.

Moral: Good manners should help you be good, not bad. ❧

Humpty Dumpty

Humpty Dumpty sat on a wall.
Humpty Dumpty had a great fall.
All the king's horses
And all the king's men
Couldn't put Humpty together again.

The **Wombat** and
the **Kangaroo**

A mother kangaroo was resting by a stream with her little joey. It was a warm afternoon. She was telling him tales about animals and gods. The joey fell asleep. The mother fell asleep, too. Suddenly they were both startled by a sad moan.

"Oh, me," groaned a strange voice, "I am sad and lonely!" The mother kangaroo looked around. She saw an old wombat by the river. He was crying. "What's wrong?" she asked him, "Why are you so sad?" The wombat said, "I have no friends. I feel old and lonely." The mother kangaroo had common sense. She said, "You just need a nice meal. Follow me. I'll take you where spear grass grows. Good mushrooms to eat are there, too. That will cheer you up." The wombat wiped away his tears. He grabbed the kangaroo's strong tail. She hopped with him to where spear grass grew by a spring. The wombat ate the grass, very contented.

Suddenly, she remembered her joey! She hopped as fast as she could back to where she left him. At first she couldn't find him, but she followed his tracks. She found him asleep in the shade of a gum tree. "He's safe," she thought, "so I had better check on the wombat. A mother's work is never done!" She hopped back to the wombat. She could hear his mouth crunching the grass when she got near. But she heard another sound, too. The soft steps of a hunter! He had spotted the wombat and was sneaking up on him. "Run, friend wombat, run!" she hollered. The old wombat took off as fast as his stubby legs could carry him.

The hunter heard the kangaroo. He chased her. She hopped away as fast as she could to a dirt cave. It was like a wombat burrow, but

bigger. She hid there and saw the hunter run by. Then she saw the hunter turn around and run the other way. And then she saw the hunter run the first way again. "He's going in two directions, like me!" she thought. This time the hunter kept going. The kangaroo hopped out of the burrow and hopped as fast as she could back to her joey. "Oh!" she cried, "I wish I could be everywhere and take care of everyone." The joey was still asleep under the gum tree. She caught her breath while he finished his nap. When he woke up, she said, "Let's go see how our friend the sad wombat is doing. I know he was scared by that hunter." They hopped back to where the spear grass grew. He wasn't there. They followed the wombat's tracks until the tracks disappeared into nowhere.

What she didn't know was that the wombat wasn't really a humble wombat. He was the great god Byamee. He had come to earth to see who had the kindest and most selfless heart. He met many creatures who were mean to him. They thought he was just an old wombat. But then Byamee found the kangaroo mother. She tried to take care of others as well as her own joey. She had the kindest heart.

Byamee wanted to give her a gift. He wanted a perfect gift for a good mother with common sense. And he wanted to be sure she couldn't lose it. A wombat has a pouch, so he decided that the kangaroo should have a pouch, too. Byamee said to his fellow gods in the sky, "Go down to earth and weave a dilly bag from grass. Make it like an apron. Then give it to the kind kangaroo. Tell her to wear it around her waist, so she never forgets it when she hops to help others."

The kangaroo mother was very happy with her new pouch. She was so happy that she put her joey in it! She thanked Byamee. Then she said, "This is a good gift for everyone with common sense. Could you give a pouch to more of my animal friends?" Byamee was glad she wanted to share her new pouch. He gave pouches to the kangaroos, the koalas, the possums—and to all the marsupials in the world. ⁕

Little
Bo Peep

Little Bo Peep has lost her sheep,
And can't tell where to find them.
Leave them alone, and they'll come home,
Wagging their tails behind them.

Little **Boy Blue**

Little Boy Blue, come blow your horn.
The sheep's in the meadow, the cow's in the corn.
Where is the boy that looks after the sheep?
He's under the haystack, fast asleep.
Will you wake him?
No, not I, for if I do he'll be sure to cry.

The *Story of* Chicken Little

When Chicken Little was in the woods one day, an acorn fell on her head. She thought that the sky was falling, so she ran to tell the King.

On the way, she met Henny Penny. "Where are you going, Chicken Little?" asked Henny Penny.

"The sky is falling, and I am going to tell the King."

"I will go with you, if I may," said Henny Penny.

And away they both ran. Soon they met Cocky Locky. "Where are you going, Henny Penny?" asked Cocky Locky.

"The sky is falling, and I am going with Chicken Little to tell the King."

"I will go with you, if I may," said Cocky Locky.

And they all ran down the road. When they came to the pond, they saw Ducky Lucky. "Where are you going, Cocky Locky?" asked Ducky Lucky.

"The sky is falling, and we are going to tell the King."

"I will go with you, if I may," said Ducky Lucky.

And away they went. Next they met Goosey Loosey. "Where are you going, Ducky Lucky?" asked Goosey Loosey.

"The sky is falling, and we are going to tell the King."

"I will go with you, if I may," said Goosey Loosey. "Let us run fast."

At the top of the hill, they met Turkey Lurkey. "Where are you going, Goosey Loosey?" asked Turkey Lurkey.

"The sky is falling, and we are going to tell the King."

"I will go with you, if I may," said Turkey Lurkey. And they all ran down the hill.

Foxy Loxy heard them coming and ran out to meet them. "Where are you going?" he asked.

"The sky is falling, and we are going to tell the King," they cried.

"Come with me, and I will show you the way," said Foxy Loxy.

So Foxy Loxy led Chicken Little, Henny Penny, Cocky Locky, Ducky Lucky, Goosey Loosey, and Turkey Lurkey across the field and through the woods.

He led them straight into his den, and they never saw the King to tell him that the sky was falling. ❧

Sing a Song of Sixpence

Sing a song of sixpence
A pocket full of rye,
Four and twenty blackbirds
Baked in a pie.

When the pie was opened,
The birds began to sing.
Wasn't that a dainty dish
To set before the king?

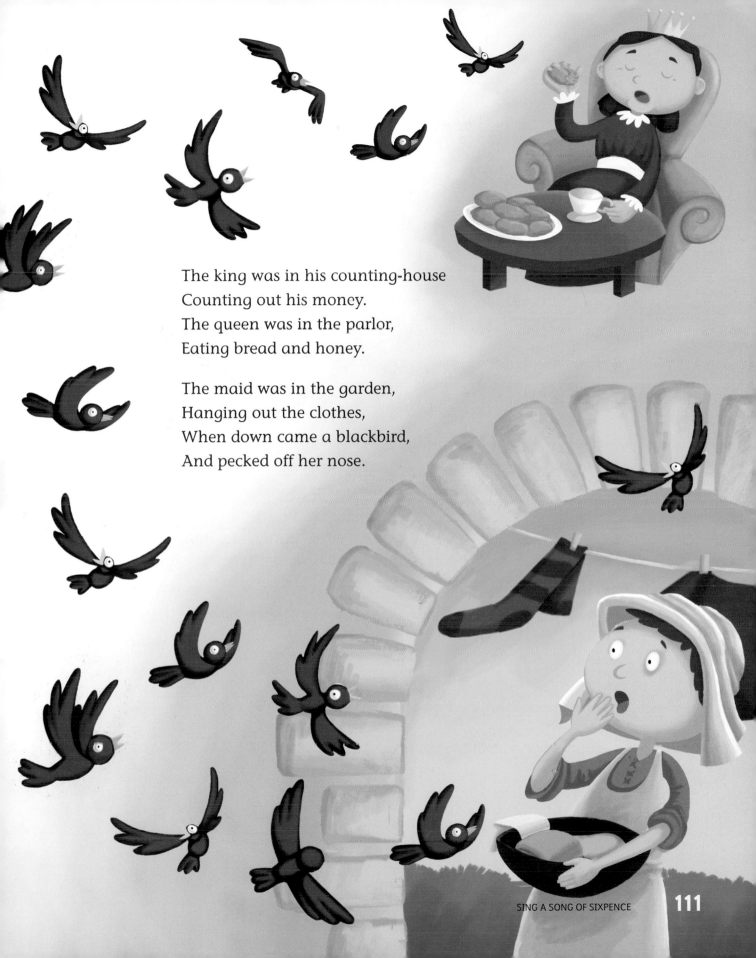

The king was in his counting-house
Counting out his money.
The queen was in the parlor,
Eating bread and honey.

The maid was in the garden,
Hanging out the clothes,
When down came a blackbird,
And pecked off her nose.

The *The* **Foolish Rabbit**

a folktale from India

Once upon a time, a rabbit was asleep under a palm tree. All at once he woke up, and thought, "What if the world should break into pieces? What would happen to me then?"

At that moment, some monkeys up in the tree dropped a coconut. It fell down on the ground, *thump-a-bump!* just behind the rabbit.

Hearing the noise, the rabbit cried, "Help! Help! The world is breaking into pieces!"

And he jumped up and ran just as fast as he could, without even looking back to see what made the noise.

Another rabbit saw him running, and called after him, "What are you running so fast for?"

"Don't ask!" he cried. "Can't stop—must run!"

But the other rabbit ran after him, begging to know what the matter was.

Then the first rabbit said, "Don't you know? The world is breaking into pieces!"

And on he ran, and the second rabbit ran with him.

Then they met another rabbit, and he too ran with them when he heard that the world was breaking into pieces.

One rabbit after another joined them, until there were hundreds of rabbits running as fast as they could go.

They passed a deer, and called out to him that the world was breaking into pieces. Then the deer ran with them, too.

The deer called out to the fox to come along because the world was breaking into pieces.

On and on they ran, and soon an elephant joined them.

At last the lion saw the animals running, and heard their cry that the world was breaking into pieces. He thought there must be some mistake, so he ran to the foot of a hill in front of them and roared three times.

They all stopped in their tracks, for they knew the voice of the king of beasts, and they feared him.

"Now," said the lion, "tell me, why are you running so fast?"

"Oh, King Lion," they answered him, "the world is breaking into pieces!"

"Who saw it breaking?" asked the lion. "You, Elephant—did you see it?"

"No, I didn't," said the elephant. "Ask the fox—he told me about it."

"I didn't see it," said the fox. "The deer told me."

"The rabbits told me about it," said the deer.

One after another of the rabbits said, "I didn't see it, but another rabbit told me about it."

At last the lion came to the rabbit who had first said the world was breaking into pieces. "Well, now," said the lion, "is it true that the world is breaking into pieces?"

"Yes, O Lion, it is," said the rabbit, his voice shaking with fright. "I was asleep under a palm tree. I woke up and thought, 'What would happen to me if the world should break into pieces?' At that very moment, I heard the sound of the world breaking up, and I ran away."

"Then," said the lion, "you and I will go back to the place where the world began to break up, and see what the matter is."

So the lion put the little rabbit on his back, and away they went like the wind. The other animals waited for them at the foot of the hill.

The rabbit told the lion when they were near the place where he slept, and the lion saw just where the rabbit had been sleeping.

He saw, too, the coconut that had fallen to the ground nearby. Then the lion said to the rabbit, "It must have been the sound of the coconut falling to the ground that you heard. You foolish rabbit!"

The lion ran back to the other animals and told them all about it. And it is good that he did, for had it not been for the wise king of beasts, they might all be running still. ❧

The **Honest Woodsman**

adapted from Emilie Poulsson

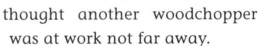

Once upon a time, out in the green, silent woods, near a rushing river that foamed and sparkled as it hurried along, there lived a good man whose work was chopping wood. One fine autumn day, he started out on his walk to the forest, with his strong, sharp ax over his shoulder. He selected a large oak tree near the riverside. He swung his ax steadily as he chopped away at the trunk.

The chips flew fast at every stroke. The sound of the ax ringing against the wood echoed so clearly you might have thought another woodchopper was at work not far away.

By and by, the woodsman thought he would rest awhile. He leaned his ax against the tree and turned to sit down. But he tripped against his ax, and before he could catch it, it slid down the bank into the river, just where the water was very deep!

The poor woodsman gazed into the stream, which flowed on over his lost ax just as merrily as before.

"Oh, what shall I do?" the woodsman cried. "My good ax!

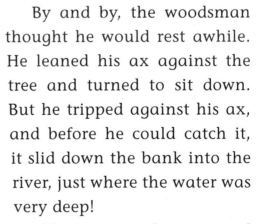

The only ax I own. So strong it was, and so sharp, and the handle worn so smooth to my hands."

Now in this river there lived a water fairy, and she heard the sad words of the woodsman. Rising to the surface, she spoke to him in a voice that was like the sweet, tuneful tinkle of flowing water.

"What is your sorrow?" she said kindly.

The woodsman, full of wonder at the sudden appearance of this lovely creature, told her of his trouble.

"Cease your sad words," said the fairy in her tinkling voice. "Far, far below lays your ax. Fairy eyes may see even in the watery depths of the stream."

She sank, and then, quick as a wink, she rose again. With her she brought an ax of silver. She held it before the woodsman's eyes and asked, "Is *this* the ax you lost?"

The woodsman knew that with so rich a treasure, he could buy many axes, and many other wonderful things besides. But he shook his head and said, "No, that is not my ax."

"Well, then," the fairy said, "here on the bank let this remain. I shall go down and try again."

She sank beneath the water, and then popped back up again. This time she held an ax of gold—the blade, the handle, all was pure, solid gold. "Is *this* the ax you lost?" she asked.

"Oh, no!" the woodsman replied. "That is not my old ax. It shines much more brightly than my old ax. It must be worth a great deal more than mine."

"Indeed!" said the fairy. "Then this golden ax may lie on the bank beside the silver one, while I seek again for yours."

The blue waters closed once again over the fairy. The woodsman looked at the gold ax and the silver ax, glittering in the grass.

"They are beautiful," he said, "and worth far more than my old ax, which is only made of wood and steel. Still, it is as good an ax as ever chopped a tree."

At this moment the water fairy again appeared, holding another ax high in the air. The woodsman reached forward with a shout of joy.

"That is mine!" he cried. "That is surely my own old ax!"

"Yes," said the fairy as she put it in his hands, "this is your ax, but it is only a plain one of wood and steel. Did you not like the silver ax and the gold ax?"

"Oh, I liked them very much!" answered the woodsman. "But the silver ax was not mine, and the gold ax was not mine. I would be wrong to say they were mine when in truth they do not belong to me."

"Honest woodsman," said the fairy with a smile, "truth is better than silver or gold. And so, farewell. But take as a gift from me the ax of silver and the ax of gold."

With that, she waved her hand and disappeared beneath the water. Greatly surprised, the woodsman stared at the river, but it only sparkled and rippled as usual.

At last, with his heart full of thanks, the honest woodsman gathered up the three axes and hurried home to tell of his wonderful adventure. ⚘

Diamonds
and Toads

adapted from the retelling by Charles Perrault

Once upon a time there was a widow who had two daughters. The elder daughter looked and acted just like her mother. They were both so disagreeable and so proud that no one enjoyed their company.

The younger daughter, however, was sweet-tempered, courteous, and lovely to look upon. But, as people naturally love their own likeness, the mother greatly favored her elder daughter. At the same time, she disliked the younger daughter, and made her do all the housework.

Among other things, twice a day this poor child had to walk half a mile, carrying a heavy pitcher, to draw water from a spring in the woods. One day, as she was at this spring, there came to her a poor woman who begged her for a drink.

"Oh, yes ma'am, with all my heart!" said this kind little girl. Quickly rinsing the pitcher, she took up some water from the clearest part of the spring and gave it to the old woman.

When the woman had finished drinking, she said, "You are so very good and kind, my dear, that I cannot help giving you a gift." For this woman, you see, was a fairy, who had taken the form of a poor country woman in order to test the kindness and good manners of the younger daughter.

"This shall be your gift," continued the fairy. "From this time forth, at every word you speak, there shall come out of your mouth either a flower or a jewel."

When the younger daughter came home, her mother scolded her for staying so long at the spring.

"I beg your pardon, Mama," said the poor girl. "I will try to do better next time." And as she spoke these words, there came out of her mouth two roses, two pearls, and two diamonds.

"What is it I see there?" said the mother, quite astonished. "I think I see pearls and diamonds come from your mouth! How can this be?"

The child told her mother all that had happened—how she met the old woman at the spring, gave her water, and was given a gift in return. As she spoke, flowers and jewels poured forth.

"To be sure," cried the mother, "I must send my elder daughter to the spring. Come here, Fanny! Look what comes from your sister's mouth when she speaks. Would you not be glad, my dear, to have the same gift given to you? All you have to do is go and draw water from the spring, and when a poor woman asks you for a drink, give it to her very kindly."

"What!" cried this rude girl. "Do you really expect me to go draw water from the spring? Send my sister to do such rough work. I will not go!"

"You shall go," said the mother, "and this minute!"

So away she went, but grumbling all the way, and taking with her the best silver pitcher in the house.

As soon as she reached the spring, she saw coming out of the wood a lady most gloriously dressed, who came up to her and asked for a drink. This was, as you know, the same fairy who had appeared to her sister, but who now appeared as a princess, to see just how far this girl's rudeness would go.

"Oh," said the proud, selfish girl, "so it's water you want? And you think I have come all this way to serve you? I suppose you think

I brought this silver pitcher for just such a fine lady as yourself. Well, if you want a drink, you can get it yourself." And she flung the pitcher on the ground at the lady's feet.

In a calm voice, the fairy said, "You are a rude and unkind child. For this, I will give you a gift fitting your actions. From this time forth, at every word you speak, snakes or toads shall fall from your mouth."

When the elder daughter returned home, her mother cried out, "Well, daughter? Did you see the old woman? And did she give you a gift?"

"Yes, indeed, mother!" answered the rude girl. And as she spoke, two vipers and two toads fell from her lips.

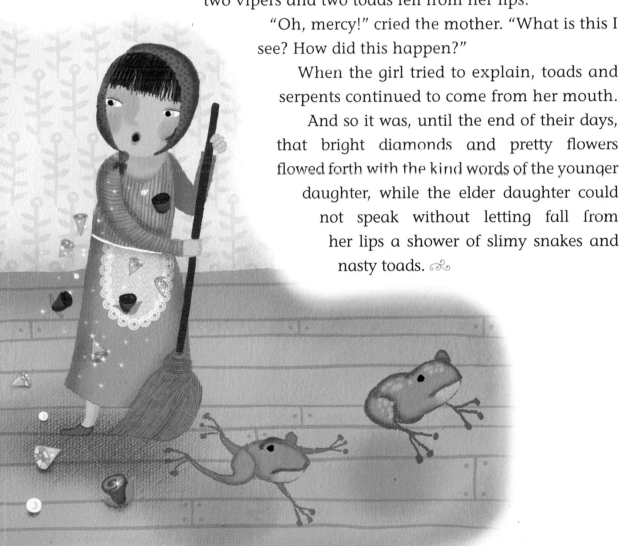

"Oh, mercy!" cried the mother. "What is this I see? How did this happen?"

When the girl tried to explain, toads and serpents continued to come from her mouth.

And so it was, until the end of their days, that bright diamonds and pretty flowers flowed forth with the kind words of the younger daughter, while the elder daughter could not speak without letting fall from her lips a shower of slimy snakes and nasty toads. ❧

Talk

a folktale from West Africa, retold by Harold Courlander and George Herzog

Once, not far from the city of Accra on the Gulf of Guinea, a country man went out to his garden to dig up some yams to take to the market.

While he was digging, one of the yams said to him:

"Well, at last you're here. You never weeded me, but now you come around with your digging stick. Go away and leave me alone!"

The farmer turned around and looked at his cow in amazement. The cow was chewing her cud and looking at him.

"Did you say something?" he asked.

The cow kept on chewing and said nothing, but the man's dog spoke up.

"It wasn't the cow who spoke to you," the dog said. "It was the yam. The yam says to leave him alone."

The man became angry, because his dog had never talked before, and he didn't like his tone besides. So he took his knife and cut a branch from a palm tree to whip his dog.

Just then the palm tree said:

"Put that branch down!"

The man was getting very upset about the way things were going, and he started to throw the palm branch away, but the palm branch said:

"Man, put me down softly!"

He put the branch down softly on a stone, and the stone said:

"Hey, take that thing off me!"

This was enough, and the frightened farmer started to run for his village. On the way, he met a fisherman going the other way with a fish trap on his head.

"What's the hurry?" the fisherman asked.

"My yam said, 'Leave me alone!' Then the dog said, 'Listen to what the yam says!' When I went to whip the dog with a palm branch, the tree said, 'Put that branch down!' Then the palm branch said, 'Do it softly!' Then the stone said, 'Take that thing off me!'"

"Is that all?" the man with the fish trap asked. "Is that so frightening?"

"Well," the man's fish trap said, "did he take it off the stone?"

"Wah!" the fisherman shouted. He threw the fish trap on the ground and began to run with the farmer, and on the trail they met a weaver with a bundle of cloth on his head.

"Where are you going in such a rush?" he asked them.

"My yam said, 'Leave me alone!'" the farmer said. "The dog said, 'Listen to what the yam says!' The tree said, 'Put that branch down!'

The branch said, 'Do it softly!' And the stone said, 'Take that thing off me!'"

"And then," the fisherman continued, "the fish trap said, 'Did he take it off?'"

"That's nothing to get excited about," the weaver said, "no reason at all."

"Oh yes it is," his bundle of cloth said. "If it happened to you, you'd run, too!"

"Wah!" the weaver shouted. He threw his bundle on the trail and started running with the other men.

They came panting to the ford in the river and found a man bathing.

"Are you chasing a gazelle?" he asked them.

The first man said breathlessly:

"My yam talked at me, and it said, 'Leave me alone!' And my dog said, 'Listen to your yam!' And when I cut myself a branch, the tree

said 'Put that branch down!' And the branch said, 'Do it softly!' And the stone said, 'Take that thing off me!'"

The fisherman panted:

"And my trap said, 'Did he?'"

The weaver wheezed:

"And my bundle of cloth said, 'You'd run, too!'"

"Is that why you're running?" the man in the river asked.

"Well, wouldn't you run if you were in their position?" the river said.

The man jumped out of the water and began to run with the others. They ran down the main street of the village to the house of the chief. The chief's servants brought his stool out, and he came and sat on it to listen to their complaints. The men began to recite their troubles.

TALK 131

"I went out to my garden to dig yams," the farmer said, waving his arms. "Then everything began to talk! My yam said, 'Leave me alone!' My dog said, 'Pay attention to your yam!' The tree said, 'Put that branch down!' The branch said, 'Do it softly!' And the stone said, 'Take it off me!'"

"And my fish trap said, 'Well, did he take it off?'" the fisherman said.

"And my cloth said, 'You'd run, too!'" the weaver said.

"And the river said the same," the bather said hoarsely, his eyes bulging.

The chief listened to them patiently, but he couldn't refrain from scowling.

"Now this is really a wild story," he said at last. "You'd better all go back to your work before I punish you for disturbing the peace."

So the men went away, and the chief shook his head and mumbled to himself, "Nonsense like that upsets the community."

"Fantastic, isn't it?" his stool said. "Imagine, a talking yam!"

Hickory, Dickory, Dock

Hickory, dickory, dock!
The mouse ran up the clock.
The clock struck one,
The mouse ran down.
Hickory, dickory, dock!

The Story of Tom Thumb

a folktale from England • adapted from James Baldwin

More than a thousand years ago in England, in the days of the great King Arthur, there lived a man named Merlin. Merlin knew so many wonderful things, and was so very wise, that people called him a wizard.

Once upon a time he was traveling across the country dressed as a poor beggar. In the evening he stopped at a farmhouse and asked if he might stay there all night, for he had walked far and was tired, and there were no inns nearby.

The farmer gave him a hearty welcome and led him into the house, while the farmer's wife brought him some milk in a wooden bowl and some brown bread on a platter.

Merlin was much pleased with their kindness, and he spent the night with them very happily. Everything about the house was neat and cozy. But still, Merlin noticed that the farmer and his wife often looked very sad and heaved deep sighs.

In the morning, Merlin said to them, "My friends, you seem to live a pleasant life in this cottage. Why, then, do you seem so unhappy?"

"Ah me!" said the poor woman, with tears in her eyes. "We are sad because we have no children. I would be the happiest woman in the world if I had a son. Why, even if the boy were no bigger than my husband's thumb, I would be satisfied."

Merlin laughed at the thought of a boy no bigger than a man's thumb. And after he had eaten a breakfast of bread and milk, he thanked the good farmer and his wife and went on his way. As he thought again of a boy no bigger than a man's thumb, his eyes twinkled merrily, and a smile brightened his face.

Within a year, the farmer's wife had a son, and he was not a bit bigger than his father's thumb. One day, as the happy mother was looking at the tiny babe and thinking how pretty he was, who should come flying in through the window but the queen of the fairies, with seven other fairies behind her. The fairy queen kissed the tiny baby and announced, "He shall be called Tom Thumb." Then she turned to the seven other fairies and sang:

> *Of an acorn cup we'll make his crown;*
> *His coat we'll weave of thistle's down;*
> *His shirt of spider's web we'll spin;*
> *For trousers, feathers warm yet thin;*
> *His shoes we'll make of mouse's skin,*
> *Tanned with the downy hair within.*

As Tom got older, he never grew any larger than his father's thumb. Still, he was a clever and brave lad. There were times, however, when his small size led to some surprising adventures.

One day when his mother was making a cake, Tom climbed up on the edge of the bowl to see how it was done. When his mother began to stir, she gave the bowl such a shake that Tom slipped and fell, head over heels, into the batter.

His mother did not see him fall in, and so she kept on stirring and stirring, while poor little Tom was covered with milk and eggs. His mouth was so full of the batter that he could not cry out. Then, to make matters worse, Tom's mother poured the batter in a pan and popped the pan into the oven to bake!

When the batter began to get hot, Tom kicked and pounded with all his might. When Tom's mother saw the pan shaking and rattling in the oven, she cried out in fright and threw the pan out the window.

Just at that time a poor wanderer came walking by. "Well now," he said, "a cake that's thrown out a window is a cake that's not wanted. And if they don't want it, why then, I'll just help them by taking it!" So he lifted the cake from the pan and put it in a basket on his back. He had not walked far when Tom finally got the batter out of his mouth and began to cry out at the top of his lungs. When the poor man heard the screams, he was so frightened that he dropped his basket and ran down the road as fast as he could go.

What a sorry-looking fellow Tom was when he crept out of the cake! He climbed out of the basket and made his way home. When his mother saw him, she cried, "Tommy, Tommy, you're a sticky mess! Tell me, my boy, what has happened?" So he told his mother all about it. Of course she was sorry, but she was glad that at least he had not drowned in the batter. She put him into a teacup and gave him a warm bath, and then laid him in bed.

Not long after this, Tom's mother went to milk her cow in the meadow, and she took him along with her. It was a very windy day, and, to keep the little fellow from being blown away, she tied him to a thistle with a piece of thread. When the cow saw little Tom's acorn-cup hat, she thought that it would be a tasty treat. So she picked poor Tom and the thistle up in a mouthful. Tom was very much afraid of her big teeth, and when she began to chew, he cried as loud as he could, "Mother! Mother!"

"Where are you, my dear Tommy?" said his mother.

"Here, mother," he said, "here I am, in the cow's mouth."

His mother cried, "Oh, my poor little boy, you shall be swallowed, for sure!" But Tom had begun to kick with all his might, until the poor cow thought she had swallowed a mad wasp. She opened her mouth and gave a loud Mooo!—and just then, lickety-split, out jumped Tom.

His mother caught him in her apron and carried him home. "Oh, Tom," she said, "I must take better care of you. I can't let you out of my sight even for a minute!"

The very next day, Tom went with his father to help drive the cows from the field. As he ran along, his foot slipped and he rolled into a ditch. Just at this moment, a great black raven swooped down and snatched Tom up in its claws. But when the bird realized that Tom was not a frog or cricket or something good to eat, it dropped poor Tom down, down, down into the deep, dark sea.

Ah, what would have become of poor Tom if it had not been for his friends the fairies? He had hardly touched the water when a big fish swallowed him and swam away. But the fish was quickly caught by a fisherman, who sold it to the servants of King Arthur. When they cut the fish open in order to cook it, they were surprised to find the tiny lad. And Tom, who had had quite enough of floating in a fish's belly, was glad to see the sun again, you can be sure!

The servants carried Tom to the king, who laughed to see the little fellow. From that day forth, whenever the king rode out on horseback, he took Tom along with him. And if the rain came on, or if the wind blew chill, Tom would creep through a buttonhole and snuggle close to the great king's heart.

One day the king asked Tom about his father and mother, and wanted to know whether they were as small as he was. "Your majesty," said Tom, "my mother and father are as tall as other people. They are good people, and kind, but they are not rich. They have very little, but they do not complain of that. Oh, your majesty," Tom cried, "I am sure they miss me, and must be greatly worried what has become of me. I beg of you that I might go and see them."

The king said that indeed, he could go, and that he should take with him as much money as he could carry. But, as Tom was so small, he could hardly lift even a single penny onto his back. So the king ordered his craftsmen to build a tiny cart, and into this cart he placed a small pile of gold coins. Two mice were harnessed to pull the tiny cart, and Tom was to walk proudly by their side.

THE STORY OF TOM THUMB

The suit of clothes that the fairies had made for Tom was now pretty well worn out, so the king gave orders that he should have another.

Of butterflies' wings his shirt was made,
His boots of a chicken's skin;
And, by fairies learned in the tailor's trade
His coat and trousers both were made,
And lined without and within.—
For a sword, a needle hung by his side;
A dapper mouse he used to ride.—
Thus strutted Tom in stately pride.

Tom's parents were very glad to see him. They wept and laughed at once, and gently hugged him, and called him all sorts of fond names. They made a bed for him in the sugar bowl, and feasted him on a hazel nut.

When the time came for Tom to go back to King Arthur, it had rained so much that he could not travel. So his mother made a little parasol of thin paper and tied him to it. Then she opened the window and gave a puff with her mouth, and the wind carried him safe over hill and dale to the king's palace.

The king was very much pleased with the tiny knight, and ordered a little chair to be made, so that Tom could sit upon his table; and he built for him a palace of gold with a door an inch wide, and fitted it for him to live in. He also gave him a coach, drawn by six small mice. And so Tom Thumb lived out his days as the smallest knight in the court of the great King Arthur. ✎

Thumbelina

adapted from Hans Christian Andersen

Once upon a time there was a little girl no bigger than her mother's thumb, and so they called her Thumbelina.

Thumbelina did not sleep in a little bed, as you might. Her bed was half of a walnut shell. When she curled up for a nap, her mother covered her with pink rose petals for blankets.

By and by, when Thumbelina had grown large enough to run about wherever she wished to go, she started for a walk one sunshiny morning. She had not gone very far when she heard something coming *hoppity-skip, hoppity-skip* behind her. She turned around, and there she saw a great big green grasshopper.

"How do you do, Thumbelina?" he said. "Wouldn't you like to go for a ride this morning?"

"I should like it very much," said Thumbelina.

"Very well, hop up on my back," said the grasshopper. So, Thumbelina hopped up on his back, and away they went, *hoppity-skip, hoppity-skip*, through the grass.

Thumbelina thought it was the finest ride she had ever had. After a while the grasshopper stopped and let her get down off his back. "Thank you, Mr. Grasshopper," said Thumbelina. "It was very good of you to take me for a ride."

"I'm glad you enjoyed it," said the grasshopper. "You may go again some day. Good-bye!" And away he went, *hoppity-skip, hoppity-skip*, through the grass, while Thumbelina went on her walk.

She walked on and on until she came to a river. As she stood on the bank, looking down into the shining water, a fish came swimming up.

"How do you do, Thumbelina?" he said.

"How do you do, Mr. Fish?" said Thumbelina.

"Wouldn't you like to go for a sail this morning?" asked the fish.

"Yes, indeed," said Thumbelina, "but there is no boat."

"Wait a moment," said the fish, and he flipped his tail, and darted away through the water. Presently he came swimming back to the bank, and in his mouth he held the stem of a lily leaf.

"Step down on this," said the fish. "It will make a fine boat."

Thumbelina stepped down on the lily leaf and sat carefully in the middle of it. The fish kept the stem in his mouth, and swam away down the stream. Overhead the birds were singing, along the bank the flowers were blooming, and over the edge of the leaf Thumbelina could see the fishes darting here and there through the water.

So they sailed and sailed down the river, until at last the fish took her back to the bank again.

"Thank you for the sail, Mr. Fish," Thumbelina said as she stepped off on to the bank. "I never had such a good time in all my life."

"I'm glad you enjoyed it, Thumbelina. Good-bye for today."

The fish darted away through the water, and Thumbelina turned to go home. Just then Mrs. Mouse came running up.

"How do you do, Thumbelina?" she said. "Won't you come home with me and see my babies?"

"I'd love to," said Thumbelina.

Mrs. Mouse's home was quite a way down under the ground. Thumbelina crept through the long, dark passageway to the cozy room in which Mrs. Mouse and her three babies lived. They all ran races up and down the long passageway, and Thumbelina tasted the dried peas that Mrs. Mouse had brought home with her.

"I think I must go home now," Thumbelina said at last, "for my mother will be wondering where I am." So she said good-bye to them all and started off home.

She had not walked very far along the path through the field when she heard something saying "Peep, peep," in a weak, sick little voice. Thumbelina looked, and there close beside her in the grass she saw a little bird. His eyes were shut, and he looked very sick.

"Why, what's the matter, little bird?" said Thumbelina.

"Oh, I have a thorn in my foot, and it does hurt so."

"Let me see," said Thumbelina. "Perhaps I can help you."

She looked carefully, and there she saw the thorn sticking in the poor bird's foot. She took her little fingers and pulled it out, as gently as she could. Then she fetched some clear, cold water and bathed the wounded foot. The bird felt so much better that he opened his eyes.

"Why, it is Thumbelina!" he said.

THUMBELINA

"How did you know my name?" said Thumbelina, in surprise.

"That's easy to explain," said the bird. "My nest is up in a tree, close beside your window. I often hear your mother calling you. But are you not a long way from home?"

"Yes, I am," said Thumbelina. "I was hurrying home when I found you."

"Well," said the bird, "if you will climb up on my back, I'll take you there, far more quickly than you can run." So Thumbelina climbed up on the bird's back.

"Hold on tight," he said, as he spread his wings and flew swiftly up above the treetops.

He went so high that sometimes they skimmed along through the clouds, and so fast that Thumbelina could hardly get her breath. But still she thought it was very wonderful, and she was not a bit afraid.

Soon the bird landed right on the windowsill of Thumbelina's own room. She climbed down off his back and thanked him for bringing her home. Then she ran away to find her mother and tell her all about the wonderful things that had happened that day.

The *Little* Red Hen

A little red hen once found a grain of wheat. "Who will help me plant this wheat?" she asked.

"I won't," said the dog.

"I won't," said the cat.

"I won't," said the pig.

"I won't," said the turkey.

"Then I will," said the little red hen. So she planted the grain of wheat.

Soon the wheat began to grow. By and by, it grew tall and ripe. "Who will help me cut this wheat?" asked the little red hen.

"I won't," said the dog.

"I won't," said the cat.

"I won't," said the pig.

"I won't," said the turkey.

"I will, then," said the little red hen. So she cut the wheat.

"Who will take this wheat to the mill to have it ground into flour?" asked the little red hen.

"I won't," said the dog.

"I won't," said the cat.

"I won't," said the pig.

"I won't," said the turkey.

"I will, then," said the little red hen. So she took the wheat to the mill.

By and by, she came back with the flour. "Who will help me bake a loaf of bread with this flour?" asked the little red hen.

"I won't," said the dog, the cat, the pig, and the turkey.

"I will, then," said the little red hen. So she baked a loaf of bread with the flour.

"Who will help me eat this bread?" asked the little red hen.

"I will!" said the dog.

"I will!" said the cat.

"I will!" said the pig.

"I will!" said the turkey.

"No, you won't," said the little red hen. "My little chicks and I are going to do that." So she called her four little chicks, and they ate the loaf of bread. ❧

The **Three Bears**

Once upon a time, there were three bears that lived in a house in the woods. One was a great big Papa Bear, one was a middle-sized Mama Bear, and one was a wee little Baby Bear.

Each bear had a dish for porridge. The great big Papa Bear had a great big dish. The middle-sized Mama Bear had a middle-sized dish. And the wee little Baby Bear had a wee little dish.

Each bear had a chair to sit in and a bed to lie on.

One morning, Mama Bear made some nice porridge. She put it into the porridge dishes. The porridge was too hot to eat, so the bears

all went out for a walk, to give their food time to get cool. They left the door open.

While they were gone, a little girl named Goldilocks came to the house. First she looked in at the window. Then she peeped in at the door. She saw no one in the house, so she walked in.

She was very glad when she saw the porridge. First she took a taste of Papa Bear's porridge, but it was too hot. Then she took a taste of Mama Bear's porridge, but that was too cold. Then she took a taste of Baby Bear's porridge. That was just right, and she liked it so well that she ate it all up!

Then she sat down in Papa Bear's chair, but that was too hard. So she sat down in Mama Bear's chair, but that was too soft. Then she sat down in Baby Bear's chair. That was just right. But she sat down so hard that the bottom of the chair fell out!

Then Little Goldilocks felt sleepy. So she went upstairs. First she lay down on Papa Bear's bed, but it was too tall. Then she lay down on Mama Bear's bed, but that was too low. So she lay down on Baby Bear's bed, and that was just right. She covered herself up and fell fast asleep.

By this time, the Three Bears thought their porridge would be cool, so they came home to breakfast.

Little Goldilocks had left Papa Bear's spoon in his porridge. "SOMEONE HAS BEEN EATING MY PORRIDGE!" said Papa Bear in his great big voice.

When Mama Bear looked at her dish, she saw that the spoon was in it, too. "Someone has been eating my porridge!" said Mama Bear in her middle-sized voice.

Then Baby Bear looked at his dish, and there was the spoon in it, but the porridge was all gone. *"Someone has been eating my porridge, and has eaten it all up!"* said Baby Bear in his wee little voice.

Then the Three Bears began to look about them. "SOMEONE HAS BEEN SITTING IN MY CHAIR!" said Papa Bear in his great big voice.

"Someone has been sitting in my chair!" said Mama Bear in her middle-sized voice.

"Someone has been sitting in my chair and has sat the bottom out of it!" said Baby Bear in his wee little voice.

The Three Bears ran upstairs. "SOMEONE HAS BEEN LYING IN MY BED!" said Papa Bear in his great big voice.

"Someone has been lying in my bed!" said Mama Bear in her middle-sized voice.

Then Baby Bear came to look at his bed. There upon the pillow was little Goldilocks, fast asleep. *"Someone has been lying in my bed— and here she is!"* said Baby Bear in his wee little voice.

Little Goldilocks had not heard the great big voice of Papa Bear because she was fast asleep. She had heard the middle-sized voice of Mama Bear, but it was only like someone speaking in a dream. But when she heard the wee little voice of Baby Bear, she sat up wide awake.

When she saw the Three Bears, she gave a cry. She jumped up and ran down the stairs. Before the Three Bears could make up their minds what to do, she ran out the door and into the woods.

And that was the last the Three Bears saw of Goldilocks. ❧

Three Billy Goats Gruff

Characters

NARRATOR

LITTLE BILLY GOAT GRUFF

SECOND BILLY GOAT GRUFF

BIG BILLY GOAT GRUFF

TROLL

NARRATOR: Once there were three billy goats. They were all named "Gruff."

LITTLE BILLY GOAT GRUFF: *(in a squeaky voice)* My name is Little Billy Goat Gruff.

SECOND BILLY GOAT GRUFF: I'm Second Billy Goat Gruff.

BIG BILLY GOAT GRUFF: *(in a deep, strong voice)* And I'm Big Billy Goat Gruff.

NARRATOR: Near the billy goats' home was a hill. At the top, there was plenty of fresh grass. The billy goats wanted to eat the grass. But to get to the hill, they had to cross a bridge over a brook. Under the bridge lived a scary troll.

TROLL: *(in a deep, scary voice)* Grrr. I'm the big, mean troll. Everyone is afraid of me!

NARRATOR: One day the three billy goats were going to the hill to eat the grass. Little Billy Goat Gruff was the first to cross the bridge. Trip-trap! Trip-trap! went the bridge softly.

TROLL: Who is that tripping on my bridge?

LITTLE BILLY GOAT GRUFF: Oh, it is just Little Billy Goat Gruff. I am going up the hill to eat the fresh grass.

TROLL: Well, I am coming to gobble you up!

LITTLE BILLY GOAT GRUFF: Oh, no! Don't take me!

TROLL: Why not?

LITTLE BILLY GOAT GRUFF: I am too little. Wait for my brother, Second Billy Goat Gruff. He is bigger than I am.

TROLL: I would like to have a bigger billy goat for supper. But I hope he comes soon. I am starting to get hungry. Well, be off with you!

NARRATOR: So Little Billy Goat Gruff went on his way. Soon Second Billy Goat Gruff came to the bridge. Trip-trap! Trip-trap! Trip-trap! went the bridge.

TROLL: Who is that tripping on my bridge?

SECOND BILLY GOAT GRUFF: Oh, it is just Second Billy Goat Gruff. I am going up the hill to eat the fresh grass.

TROLL: Well, I am coming to gobble you up!

SECOND BILLY GOAT GRUFF: Oh, no! Don't take me!

TROLL: Why not?

SECOND BILLY GOAT GRUFF: I am not very big. Wait for my brother, Big Billy Goat Gruff. He is bigger than I am.

TROLL: I would like a really big, tasty billy goat for supper. But I hope he comes soon. I am getting *very* hungry. Well, be off with you!

NARRATOR: So Second Billy Goat Gruff went on his way. Just then Big Billy Goat Gruff came to the bridge. TRIP-TRAP! TRIP-TRAP! TRIP-TRAP! TRIP-TRAP! went the bridge loudly.

TROLL: Who is that tripping on my bridge?

BIG BILLY GOAT GRUFF: Oh, it is just Big Billy Goat Gruff. I am going up the hill to eat the fresh grass.

TROLL: Well, I am coming to gobble you up!

NARRATOR: Big Billy Goat Gruff was not afraid of the troll.

BIG BILLY GOAT GRUFF: Come along, then, Troll!

NARRATOR: So the troll came along. Big Billy Goat Gruff flew at him. The big goat caught the troll on his horns. Then he threw the troll into the brook. The troll was frightened. He jumped out of

the water and ran away. The three billy goats never saw the troll again. Now they go up the hill every day to eat fresh grass.

LITTLE BILLY GOAT GRUFF, SECOND BILLY GOAT GRUFF, AND BIG BILLY GOAT GRUFF: Munch, munch, munch.

NARRATOR: The billy goats eat so much grass on their hill that they are getting fat.

LITTLE BILLY GOAT GRUFF, SECOND BILLY GOAT GRUFF, AND BIG BILLY GOAT GRUFF: The end! ⌘

The Three Little Pigs

There was once a Mother Pig who had three little pigs. One day Mother Pig said to her three little pigs, "You must all go away and seek your fortune."

"Very well, Mother dear," said the three little pigs. And away they went to seek their fortune.

Very soon the first little pig met a man with some straw. "Please, sir," he said, "give me some straw to build a house with."

"Very well," said the man, "I will give you some straw."

So the first little pig built his house of straw.

Very soon the Big Bad Wolf came to the first little pig's house. He knocked at the door and said, "Little pig, little pig, let me come in."

"No, no," said the pig, "not by the hair of my chinny, chin, chin."

"Then," said the wolf, "I'll huff and I'll puff, and I'll blow your house in!"

And the wolf huffed and puffed and blew the house into bits of straw.

The first little pig ran and ran.

Then the second little pig met a man with some bundles of sticks. "Please, sir," he said, "give me some sticks to build a house with."

"Very well," said the man, "you may have some sticks."

So the second little pig built his house of sticks.

Very soon the Big Bad Wolf came to the second little pig's house. He knocked at the door and said, "Little pig, little pig, let me come in."

"No, no, not by the hair of my chinny, chin, chin."

"Then I'll huff and I'll puff, and I'll blow your house in!"

So he huffed and he puffed, and he blew the house in.

The second little pig ran and ran.

Then the third little pig met a man with some bricks. "Please, sir," he said, "give me some bricks to build a house with."

"Very well," said the man, "you may have some bricks."

So the third little pig built his house of bricks.

Very soon the Big Bad Wolf came to the third little pig's house. He knocked at the door and said, "Little pig, little pig, let me come in."

"No, no, not by the hair of my chinny, chin, chin."

"Then I'll huff and I'll puff, and I'll blow your house in!"

So he huffed and he puffed, and he puffed and he huffed, but he could not blow the house in.

Then the Big Bad Wolf said, "Oh, little pig, I know where to get some nice, big, red apples. Be ready tomorrow morning at five o'clock."

"Very well," said the third little pig, "I will be ready."

But the third little pig got up at four o'clock and went for the apples. He filled his pail with them. Then he went home.

At five o'clock the Big Bad Wolf came. "Are you ready, little pig?" he asked.

"See this pail of nice red apples?" said the third little pig. "I got up at four o'clock and picked them."

This made the Big Bad Wolf very angry, and he growled, *"Grr! Grr!* I am going to eat you, little pig!" So he climbed up on the roof and went down through the chimney.

The third little pig had a big pot of hot water on the fire. The Big Bad Wolf fell into the hot water. *"Ow! Ow! Ow!"* he yelled. He jumped from the pot and ran out of the house.

The first little pig and the second little pig came to live with their brother in the house of bricks. And they never saw the wolf again. ᕙ

Three **Little** **Kittens**

Three little kittens lost their mittens,
And they began to cry,
"Oh mother dear,
We sadly fear,
Our mittens we have lost."
"Lost your mittens?
You naughty kittens,
Then you shall have no pie."
"Mee-ow, mee-ow, mee-ow."
"No, you shall have no pie."
"Mee-ow, mee-ow, mee-ow."

The three little kittens found their mittens,
And they began to cry,
"Oh mother dear,
See here, see here!
Our mittens we have found!"
"Found your mittens,
You little kittens,
Then you may have some pie."
"Purr-r, purr-r, purr-r,
Oh, let us have the pie!
Purr-r, purr-r, purr-r."

The three little kittens put on their mittens
And soon ate up the pie.
"Oh mother dear,
We greatly fear
Our mittens we have soiled!"
"Soiled your mittens?
You naughty kittens!"
Then they began to sigh,
"Mee-ow, mee-ow, mee-ow."
Then they began to sigh,
"Mee-ow, mee-ow, mee-ow."

The three little kittens washed their mittens
And hung them out to dry.
"Oh, mother dear,
Look here! Look here!
Our mittens we have washed."
"Washed your mittens?
You darling kittens!
But I smell a rat close by.
Hush, hush! *Mee-ow, mee-ow.*"
"We smell a rat close by.
Mee-ow, mee-ow, mee-ow."